# the GARFIELD show

**PAPERCUT**Z™

# GARFIELD GRAPHIC NOVELS AVAILABLE FROM PAPERCUTZ ™

GARFIELD & Co #1
"FISH TO FRY"

GARFIELD & Co #2
"THE CURSE OF
THE CAT PEOPLE"

GARFIELD & Co #3
"CATZILLA"

GARFIELD & Co #4
"CAROLING CAPERS"

GARFIELD & Co #5
"A GAME OF CAT
AND MOUSE"

GARFIELD & Co #6
"MOTHER GARFIELD"

GARFIELD & Co #7
"HOME FOR THE
HOLIDAYS"

GARFIELD & Co #8
"SECRET AGENT X"

THE GARFIELD SHOW #1
"UNFAIR WEATHER"

THE GARFIELD SHOW #2
"JON'S NIGHT OUT"

THE GARFIELD SHOW #3
"LONG LOST LYMAN"

THE GARFIELD SHOW #4
"LITTLE TROUBLE IN
BIG CHINA"

THE GARFIELD SHOW #5
"FIDO FOOD FELINE"

**COMING SOON!**

THE GARFIELD SHOW #6
"STINK, STANK, STUNK"

# the GARFIELD show

## #5 "FIDO FOOD FELINE"

BASED ON THE ORIGINAL CHARACTERS CREATED BY

### JIM DAVIS

**PAPERCUTZ**™
NEW YORK

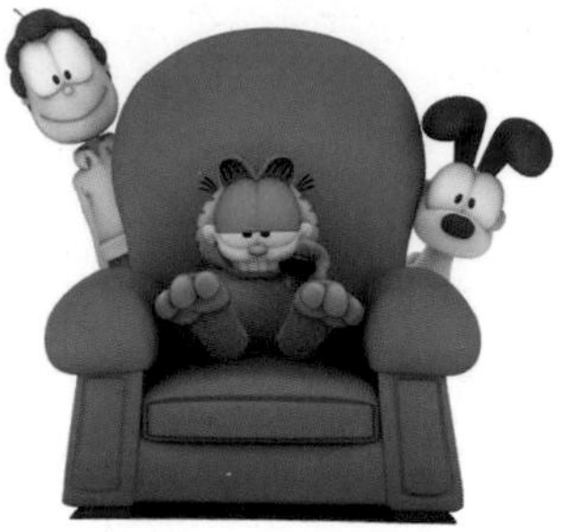

"THE GARFIELD SHOW #5 "FIDO FOOD FELINE"


IN ASSOCIATION WITH FRANCE3 WITH THE PARTICIPATION OF CENTRE NATIONAL
DE LA CINÉMATOGRAPHIE AND THE SUPPORT OF REGION ILE-DE-FRANCE.
A SERIES DEVELOPED BY PHILIPPE VIDAL, ROBERT REA AND STEVE BALISSAT.
BASED UPON THE CHARACTERS CREATED BY JIM DAVIS. ORIGINAL STORIES:
"MUSCLE MOUSE" WRITTEN BY PETER BERTS; "FITNESS CRAZED," "FIDO FOOD
FELINE," AND "THE CAPED AVENGER STRIKES AGAIN" WRITTEN BY MARK
EVANIER; "THE MOLE EXPRESS" WRITTEN BY EMMANUELLE AUBERT.

CEDRIC MICHIELS - COMICS ADAPTATION
JOE JOHNSON - TRANSLATIONS
TONY ISABELLA - DIALOGUE RESTORATION
TOM ORZECHOWSKI - LETTERING
JEFF WHITMAN - PRODUCTION COORDINATOR
SUZANNAH ROWNTREE - ASSOCIATE EDITOR
JIM SALICRUP
EDITOR-IN-CHIEF

ISBN: 978-1-62991-209-7 PAPERBACK EDITION
ISBN: 978-1-62991-210-3 HARDCOVER EDITION

PRINTED IN CHINA
MAY 2015 BY O.G. PRINTING PRODUCTIONS, LTD.
UNITS 2 & 3, 5/F, LEMMI CENTRE
50 HOI YUEN ROAD
KWON TONG, KOWLOON

PAPERCUTZ BOOKS MAY BE PURCHASED FOR BUSINESS OR PROMOTIONAL USE. FOR INFORMATION ON
BULK PURCHASES PLEASE CONTACT MACMILLAN CORPORATE AND PREMIUM SALES DEPARTMENT AT
(800) 221-7945 X5442.

DISTRIBUTED BY MACMILLAN
FIRST PAPERCUTZ PRINTING

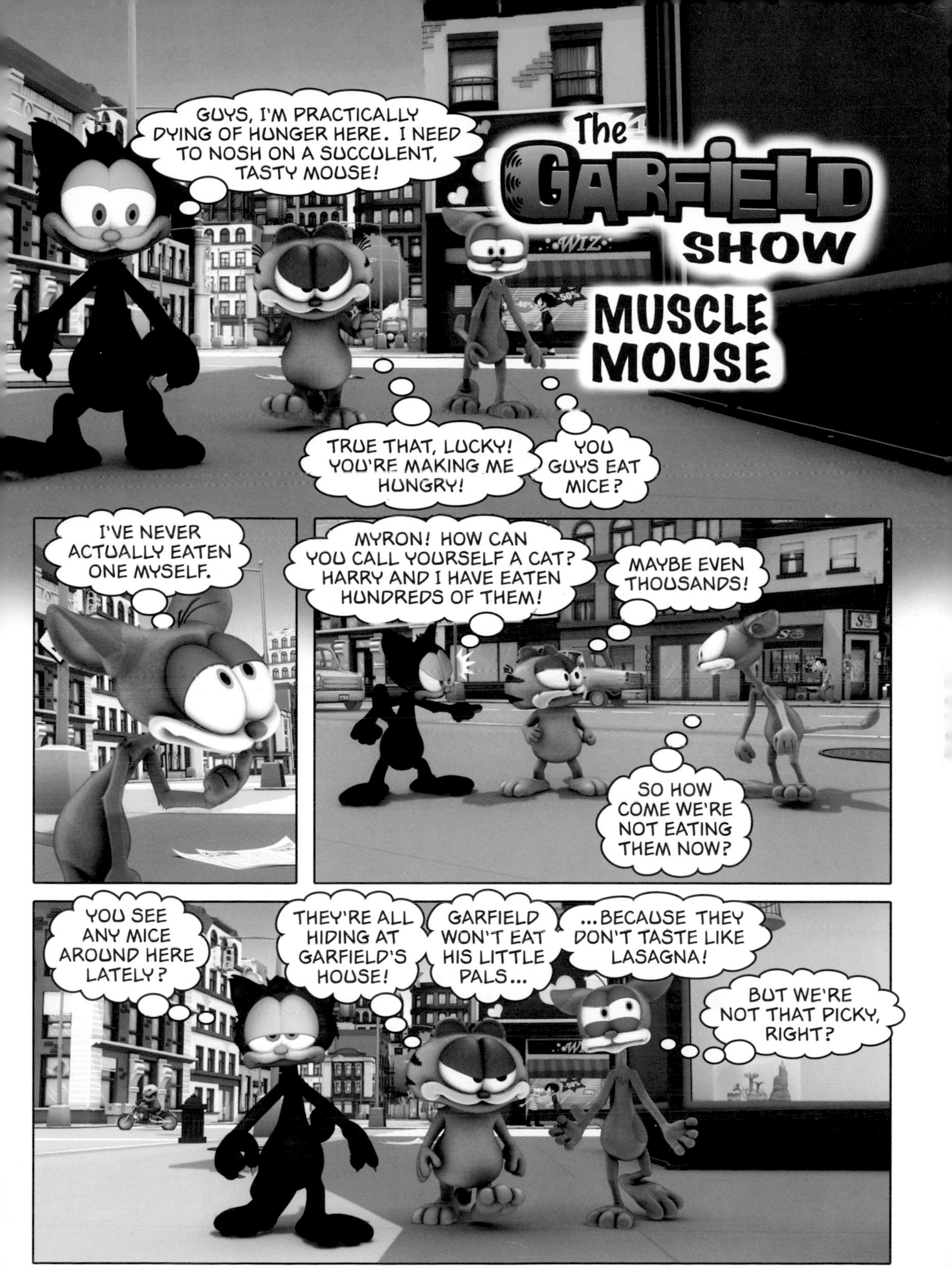
The GARFIELD SHOW
MUSCLE MOUSE
GUYS, I'M PRACTICALLY DYING OF HUNGER HERE. I NEED TO NOSH ON A SUCCULENT, TASTY MOUSE!
TRUE THAT, LUCKY! YOU'RE MAKING ME HUNGRY!
YOU GUYS EAT MICE?
I'VE NEVER ACTUALLY EATEN ONE MYSELF.
MYRON! HOW CAN YOU CALL YOURSELF A CAT? HARRY AND I HAVE EATEN HUNDREDS OF THEM!
MAYBE EVEN THOUSANDS!
SO HOW COME WE'RE NOT EATING THEM NOW?
YOU SEE ANY MICE AROUND HERE LATELY?
THEY'RE ALL HIDING AT GARFIELD'S HOUSE!
GARFIELD WON'T EAT HIS LITTLE PALS...
...BECAUSE THEY DON'T TASTE LIKE LASAGNA!
BUT WE'RE NOT THAT PICKY, RIGHT?

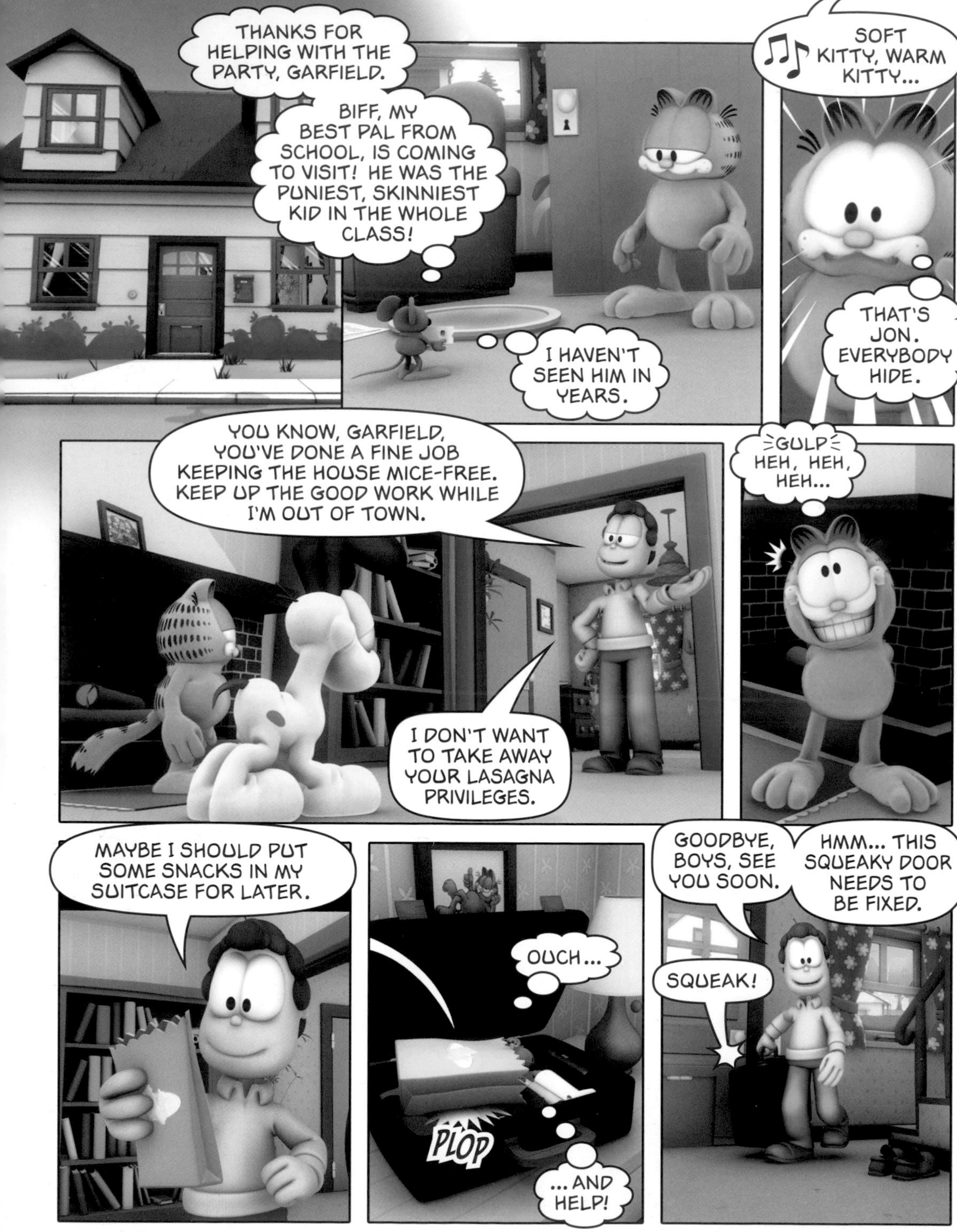
THANKS FOR HELPING WITH THE PARTY, GARFIELD.
BIFF, MY BEST PAL FROM SCHOOL, IS COMING TO VISIT! HE WAS THE PUNIEST, SKINNIEST KID IN THE WHOLE CLASS!
I HAVEN'T SEEN HIM IN YEARS.
SOFT KITTY, WARM KITTY...
THAT'S JON. EVERYBODY HIDE.
YOU KNOW, GARFIELD, YOU'VE DONE A FINE JOB KEEPING THE HOUSE MICE-FREE. KEEP UP THE GOOD WORK WHILE I'M OUT OF TOWN.
I DON'T WANT TO TAKE AWAY YOUR LASAGNA PRIVILEGES.
GULP
HEH, HEH, HEH...
MAYBE I SHOULD PUT SOME SNACKS IN MY SUITCASE FOR LATER.
OUCH...
PLOP
...AND HELP!
GOODBYE, BOYS, SEE YOU SOON.
HMM... THIS SQUEAKY DOOR NEEDS TO BE FIXED.
SQUEAK!

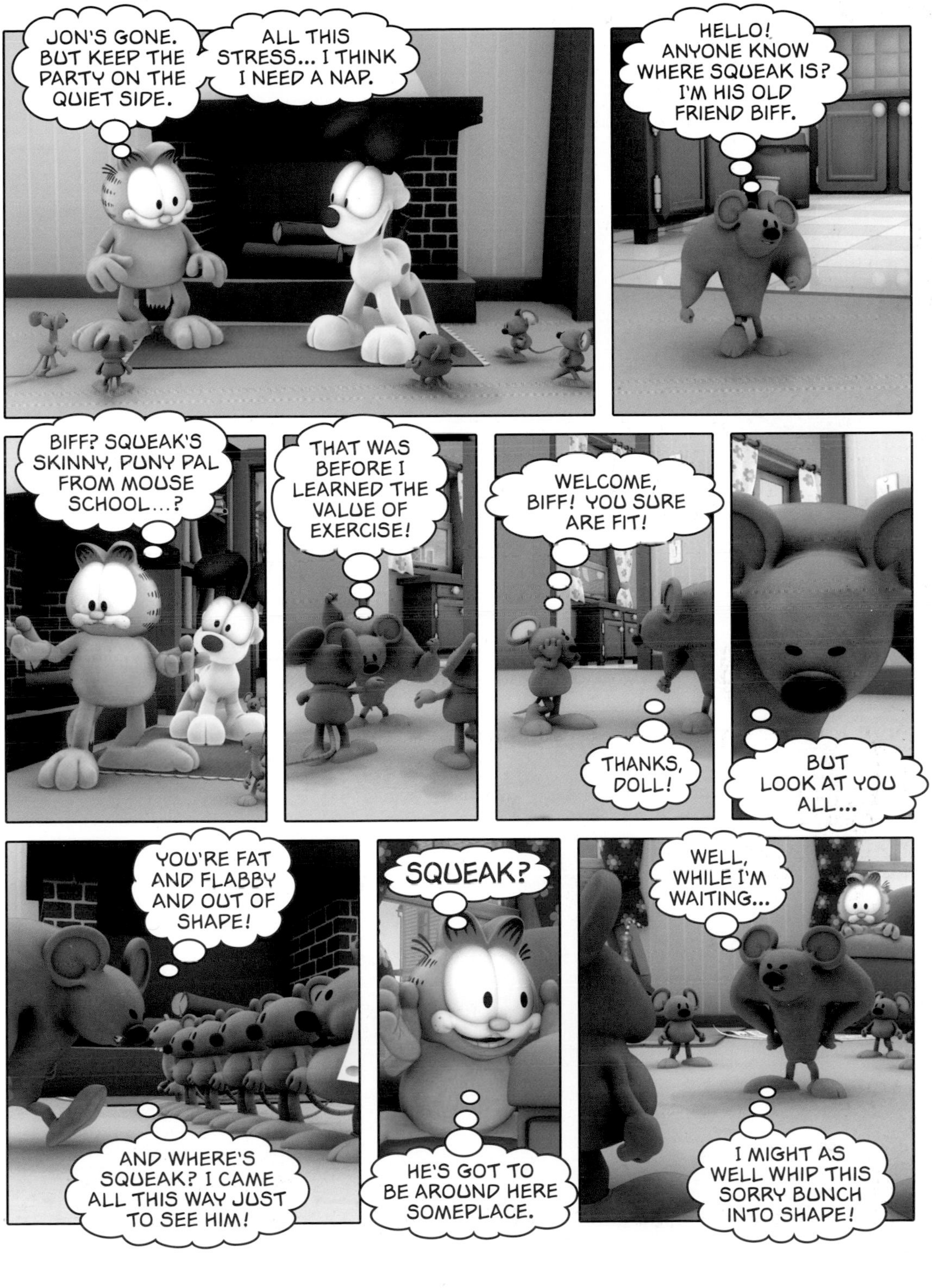
JON'S GONE. BUT KEEP THE PARTY ON THE QUIET SIDE.
ALL THIS STRESS... I THINK I NEED A NAP.
HELLO! ANYONE KNOW WHERE SQUEAK IS? I'M HIS OLD FRIEND BIFF.
BIFF? SQUEAK'S SKINNY, PUNY PAL FROM MOUSE SCHOOL...?
THAT WAS BEFORE I LEARNED THE VALUE OF EXERCISE!
WELCOME, BIFF! YOU SURE ARE FIT!
THANKS, DOLL!
BUT LOOK AT YOU ALL...
YOU'RE FAT AND FLABBY AND OUT OF SHAPE!
AND WHERE'S SQUEAK? I CAME ALL THIS WAY JUST TO SEE HIM!
SQUEAK?
HE'S GOT TO BE AROUND HERE SOMEPLACE.
WELL, WHILE I'M WAITING...
I MIGHT AS WELL WHIP THIS SORRY BUNCH INTO SHAPE!

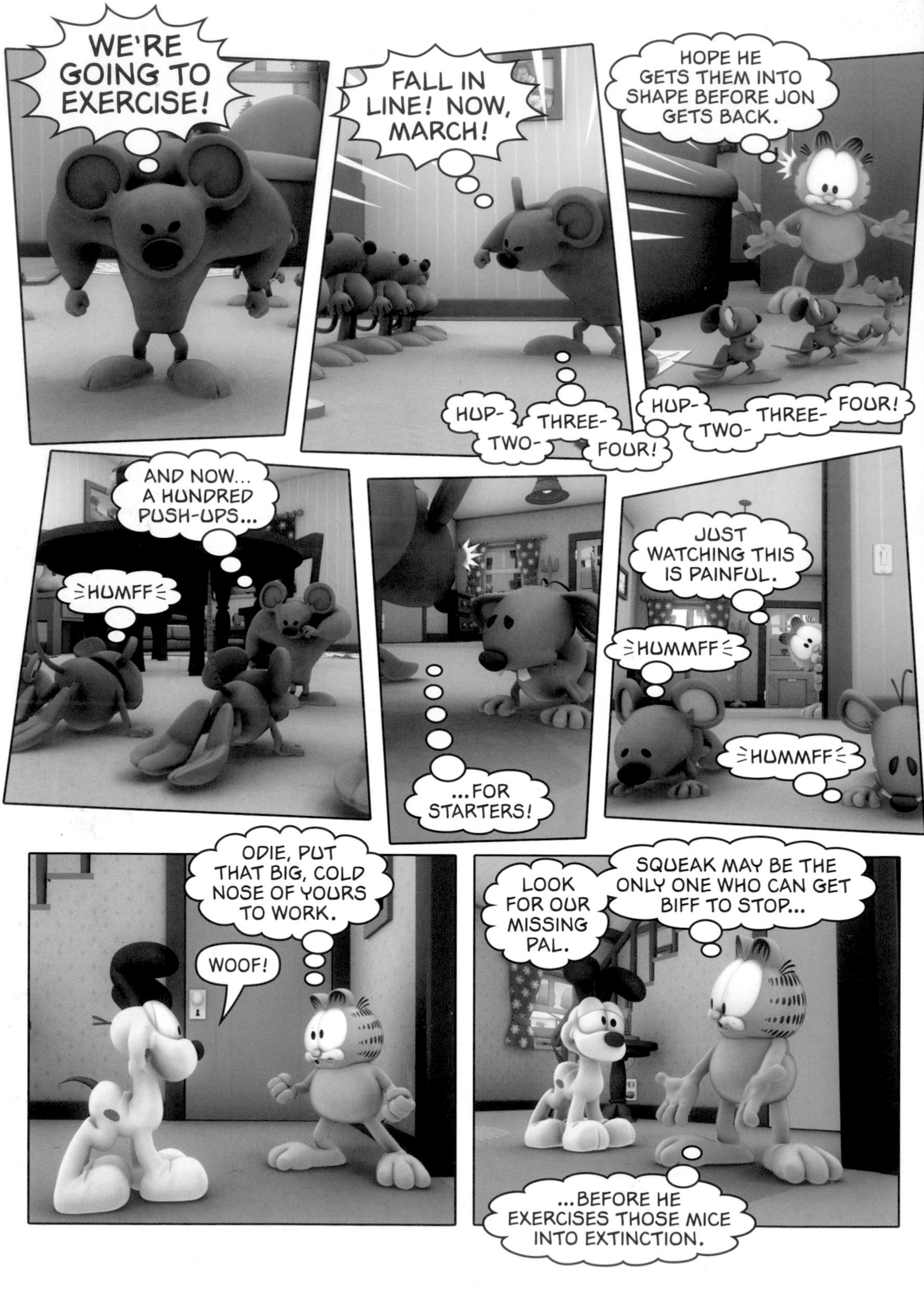

WE'RE GOING TO EXERCISE!
FALL IN LINE! NOW, MARCH!
HUP- TWO- THREE- FOUR!
HOPE HE GETS THEM INTO SHAPE BEFORE JON GETS BACK.
HUP- TWO- THREE- FOUR!
AND NOW... A HUNDRED PUSH-UPS...
HUMFF
...FOR STARTERS!
JUST WATCHING THIS IS PAINFUL.
HUMMFF
HUMMFF
ODIE, PUT THAT BIG, COLD NOSE OF YOURS TO WORK.
WOOF!
LOOK FOR OUR MISSING PAL.
SQUEAK MAY BE THE ONLY ONE WHO CAN GET BIFF TO STOP...
...BEFORE HE EXERCISES THOSE MICE INTO EXTINCTION.

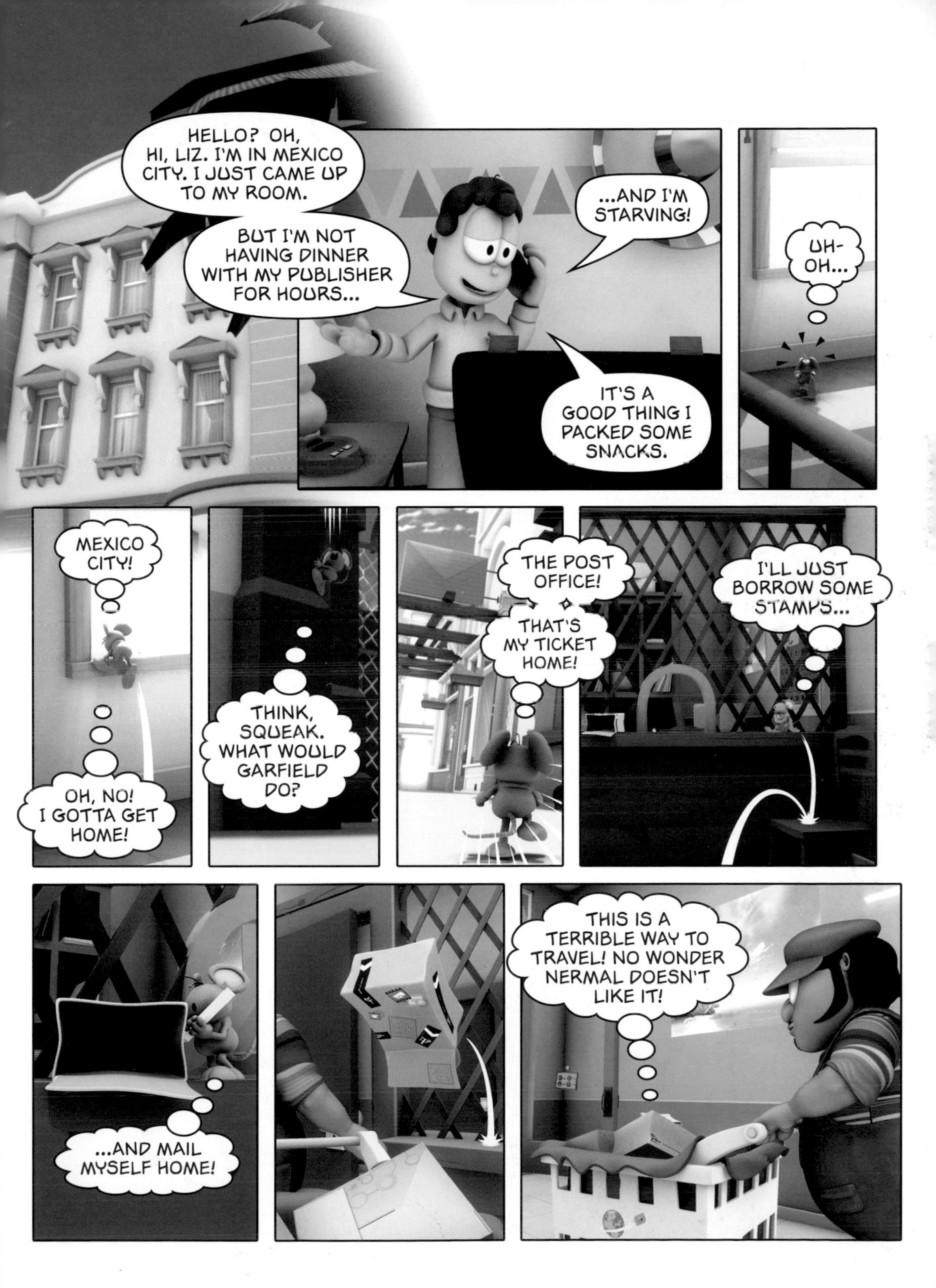
HELLO? OH, HI, LIZ. I'M IN MEXICO CITY. I JUST CAME UP TO MY ROOM.
BUT I'M NOT HAVING DINNER WITH MY PUBLISHER FOR HOURS...
...AND I'M STARVING!
IT'S A GOOD THING I PACKED SOME SNACKS.
UH-OH...
MEXICO CITY!
OH, NO! I GOTTA GET HOME!
THINK, SQUEAK. WHAT WOULD GARFIELD DO?
THE POST OFFICE!
THAT'S MY TICKET HOME!
I'LL JUST BORROW SOME STAMPS...
...AND MAIL MYSELF HOME!
THIS IS A TERRIBLE WAY TO TRAVEL! NO WONDER NERMAL DOESN'T LIKE IT!

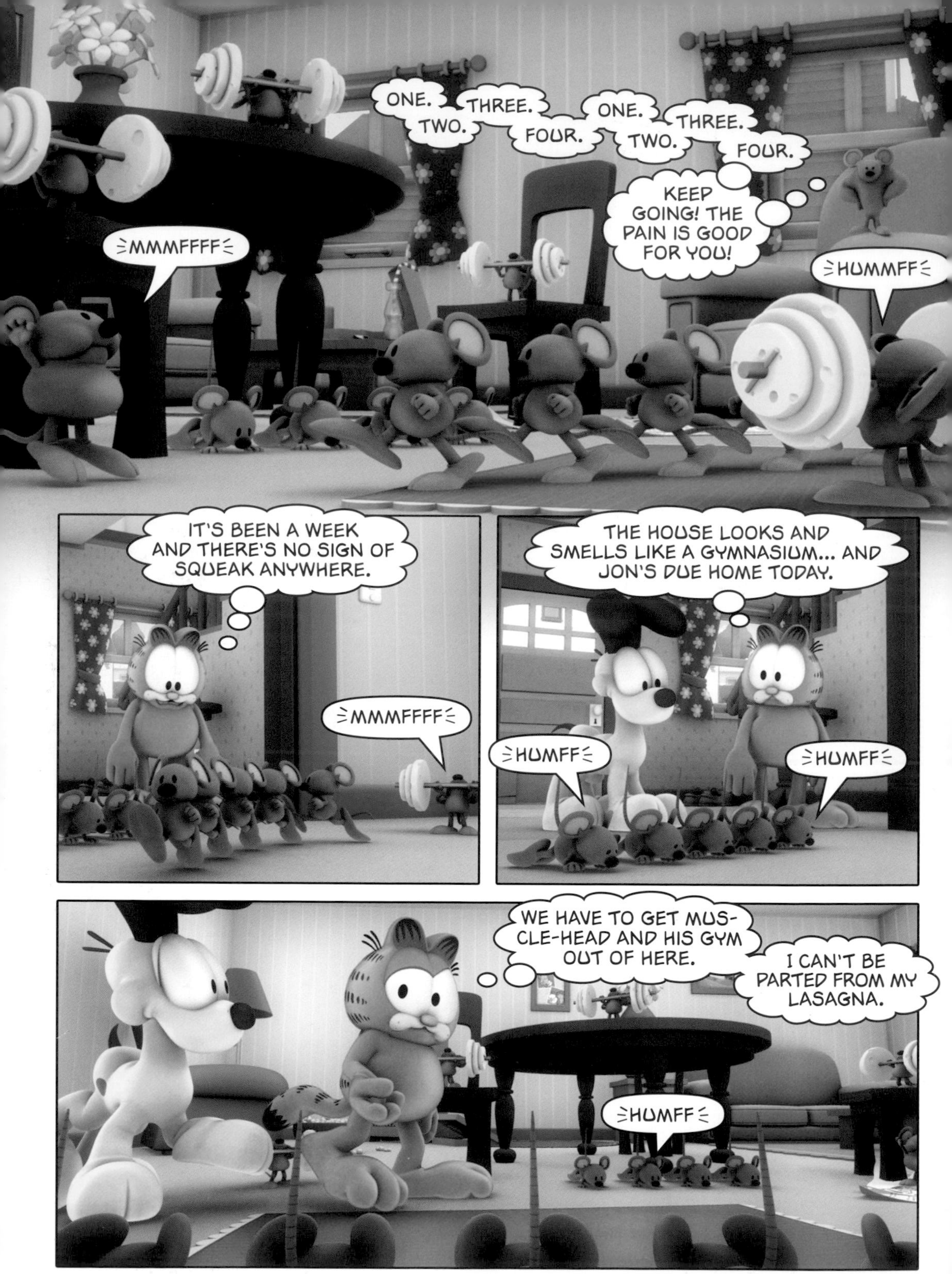
ONE.
TWO.
THREE.
FOUR.
ONE.
TWO.
THREE.
FOUR.
KEEP GOING! THE PAIN IS GOOD FOR YOU!
MMMFFFF
HUMMFF
IT'S BEEN A WEEK AND THERE'S NO SIGN OF SQUEAK ANYWHERE.
MMMFFFF
THE HOUSE LOOKS AND SMELLS LIKE A GYMNASIUM... AND JON'S DUE HOME TODAY.
HUMFF
HUMFF
WE HAVE TO GET MUS-CLE-HEAD AND HIS GYM OUT OF HERE.
I CAN'T BE PARTED FROM MY LASAGNA.
HUMFF

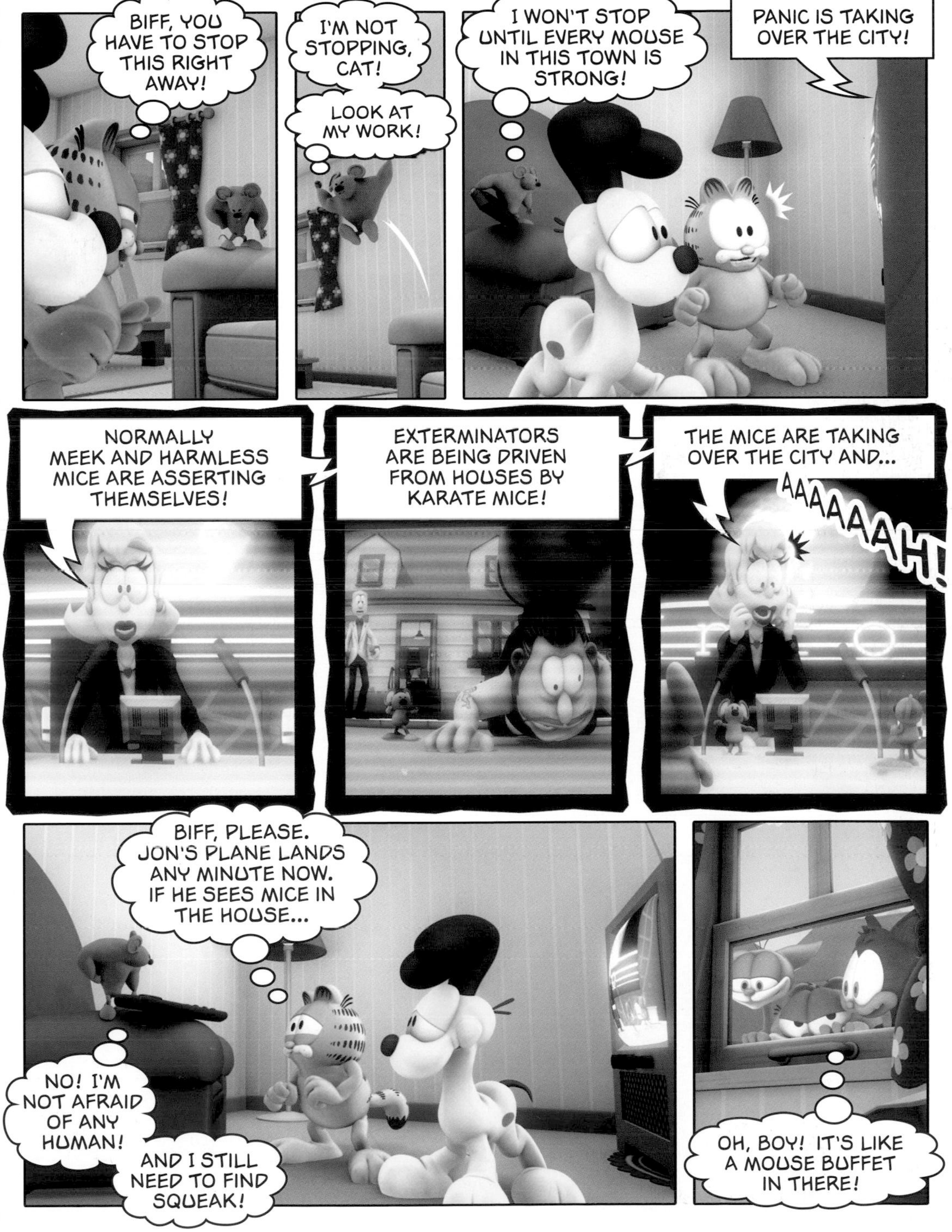
BIFF, YOU HAVE TO STOP THIS RIGHT AWAY!
I'M NOT STOPPING, CAT!
LOOK AT MY WORK!
I WON'T STOP UNTIL EVERY MOUSE IN THIS TOWN IS STRONG!
PANIC IS TAKING OVER THE CITY!
NORMALLY MEEK AND HARMLESS MICE ARE ASSERTING THEMSELVES!
EXTERMINATORS ARE BEING DRIVEN FROM HOUSES BY KARATE MICE!
THE MICE ARE TAKING OVER THE CITY AND...
AAAAAAAH!
BIFF, PLEASE. JON'S PLANE LANDS ANY MINUTE NOW. IF HE SEES MICE IN THE HOUSE...
NO! I'M NOT AFRAID OF ANY HUMAN!
AND I STILL NEED TO FIND SQUEAK!
OH, BOY! IT'S LIKE A MOUSE BUFFET IN THERE!

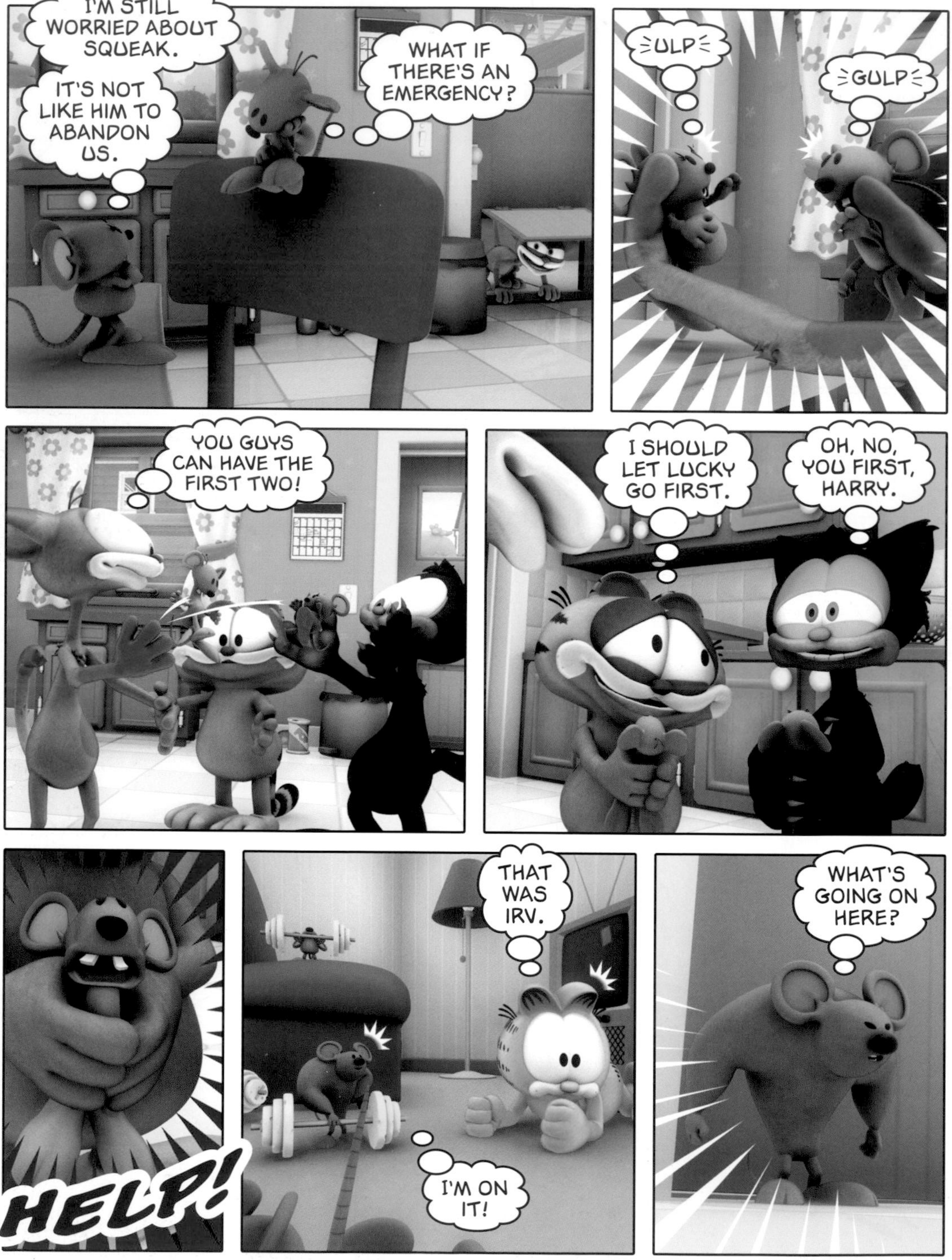
I'M STILL WORRIED ABOUT SQUEAK.
IT'S NOT LIKE HIM TO ABANDON US.
WHAT IF THERE'S AN EMERGENCY?
ULP
GULP
YOU GUYS CAN HAVE THE FIRST TWO!
I SHOULD LET LUCKY GO FIRST.
OH, NO, YOU FIRST, HARRY.
HELP!
THAT WAS IRV.
I'M ON IT!
WHAT'S GOING ON HERE?

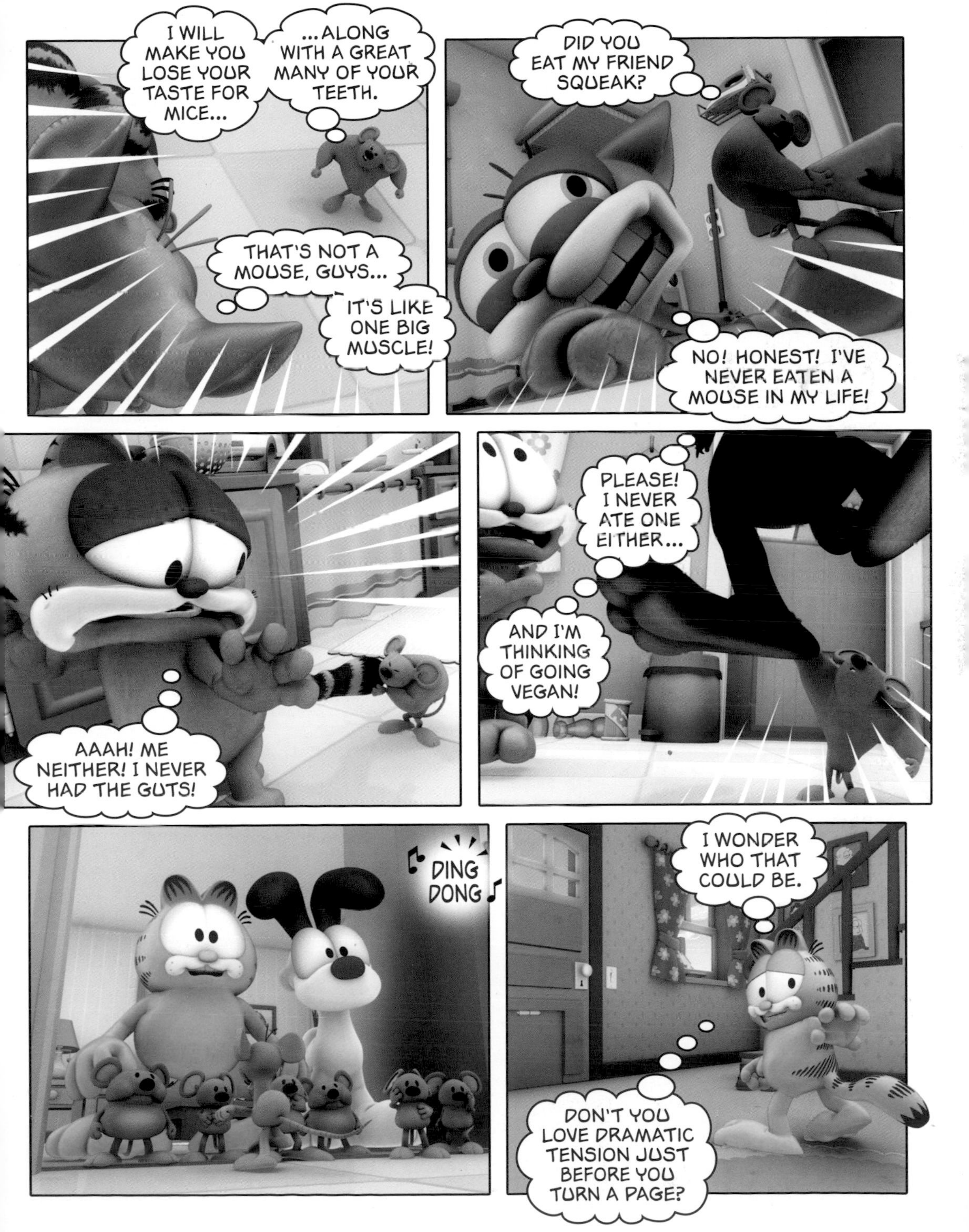
I WILL MAKE YOU LOSE YOUR TASTE FOR MICE...
...ALONG WITH A GREAT MANY OF YOUR TEETH.
THAT'S NOT A MOUSE, GUYS...
IT'S LIKE ONE BIG MUSCLE!
DID YOU EAT MY FRIEND SQUEAK?
NO! HONEST! I'VE NEVER EATEN A MOUSE IN MY LIFE!
AAAH! ME NEITHER! I NEVER HAD THE GUTS!
PLEASE! I NEVER ATE ONE EITHER...
AND I'M THINKING OF GOING VEGAN!
DING DONG
I WONDER WHO THAT COULD BE.
DON'T YOU LOVE DRAMATIC TENSION JUST BEFORE YOU TURN A PAGE?

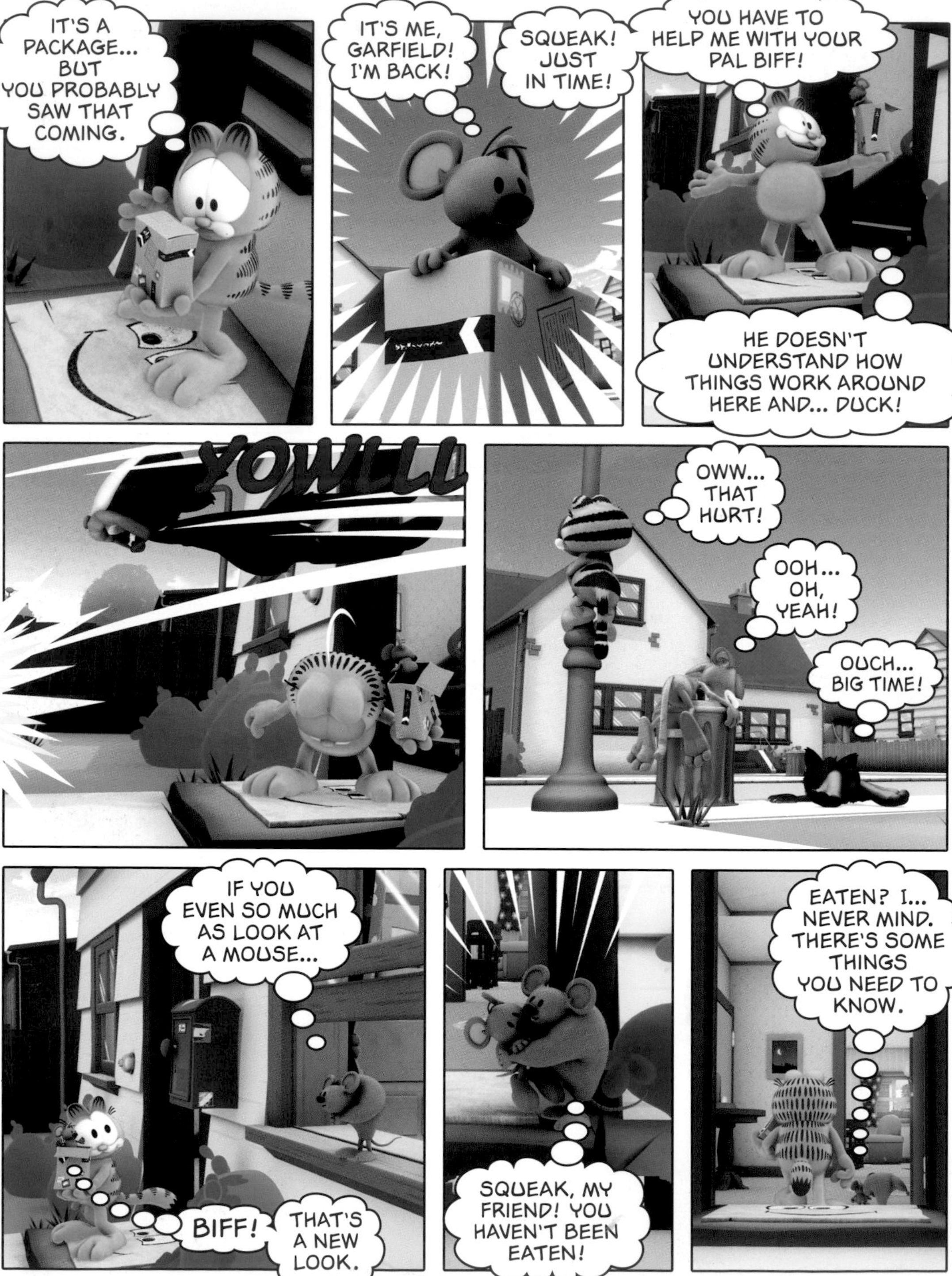
IT'S A PACKAGE... BUT YOU PROBABLY SAW THAT COMING.
IT'S ME, GARFIELD! I'M BACK!
SQUEAK! JUST IN TIME!
YOU HAVE TO HELP ME WITH YOUR PAL BIFF!
HE DOESN'T UNDERSTAND HOW THINGS WORK AROUND HERE AND... DUCK!
YOWLLL
OWW... THAT HURT!
OOH... OH, YEAH!
OUCH... BIG TIME!
IF YOU EVEN SO MUCH AS LOOK AT A MOUSE...
BIFF!
THAT'S A NEW LOOK.
SQUEAK, MY FRIEND! YOU HAVEN'T BEEN EATEN!
EATEN? I... NEVER MIND. THERE'S SOME THINGS YOU NEED TO KNOW.

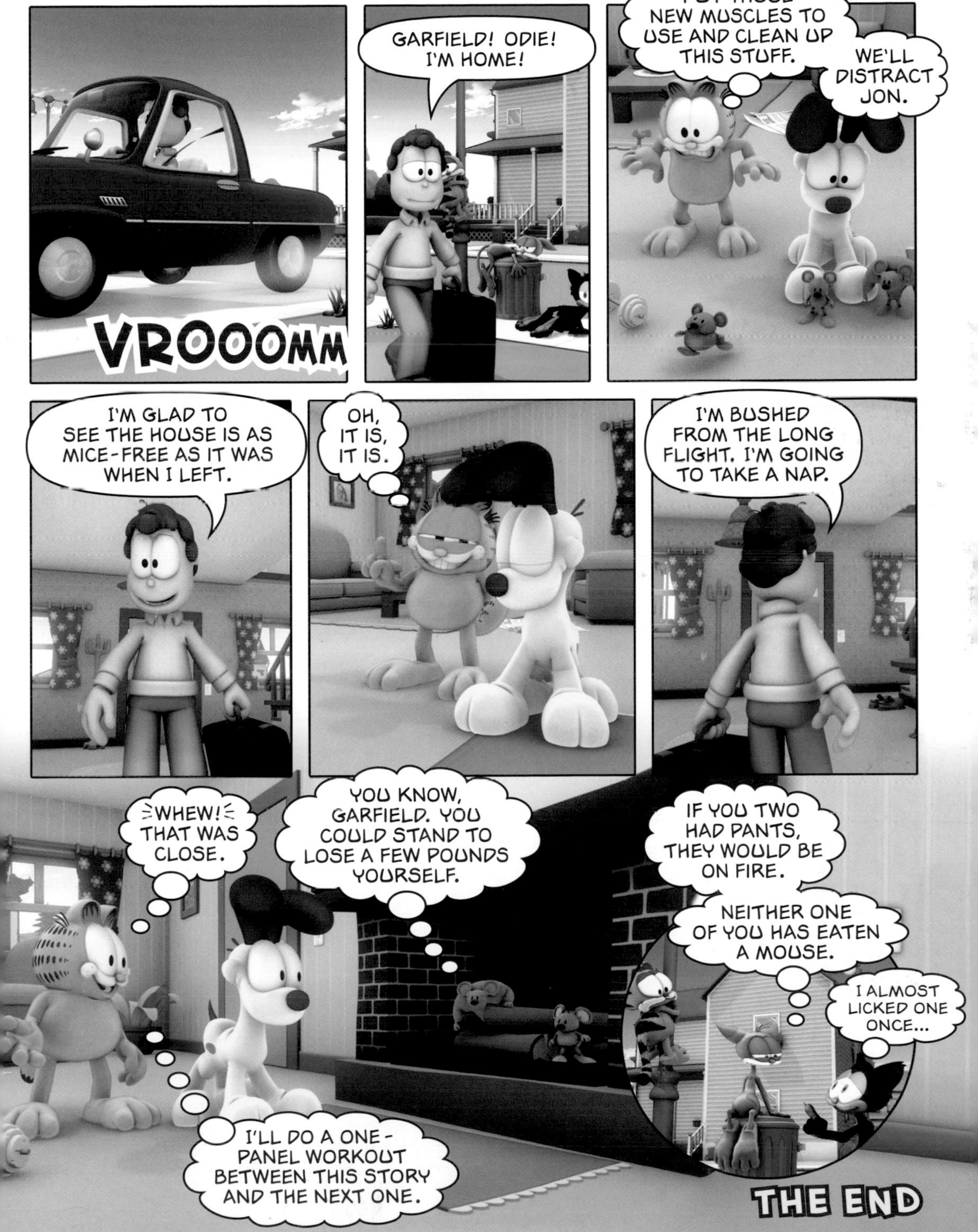
VROOOMM
GARFIELD! ODIE! I'M HOME!
PUT THOSE NEW MUSCLES TO USE AND CLEAN UP THIS STUFF.
WE'LL DISTRACT JON.
I'M GLAD TO SEE THE HOUSE IS AS MICE-FREE AS IT WAS WHEN I LEFT.
OH, IT IS, IT IS.
I'M BUSHED FROM THE LONG FLIGHT. I'M GOING TO TAKE A NAP.
WHEW! THAT WAS CLOSE.
YOU KNOW, GARFIELD. YOU COULD STAND TO LOSE A FEW POUNDS YOURSELF.
I'LL DO A ONE-PANEL WORKOUT BETWEEN THIS STORY AND THE NEXT ONE.
IF YOU TWO HAD PANTS, THEY WOULD BE ON FIRE.
NEITHER ONE OF YOU HAS EATEN A MOUSE.
I ALMOST LICKED ONE ONCE...
THE END

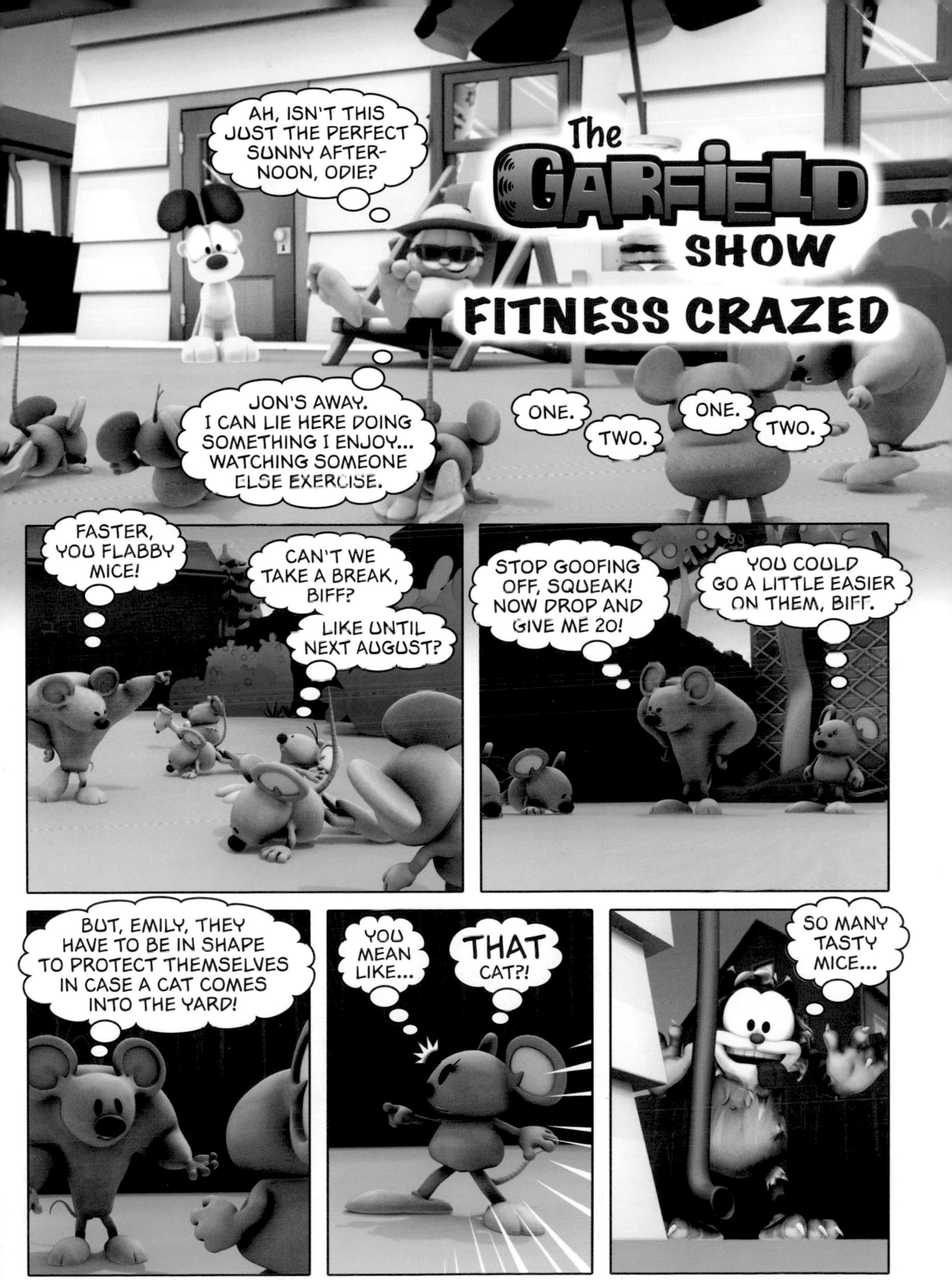
The GARFIELD SHOW
FITNESS CRAZED
AH, ISN'T THIS JUST THE PERFECT SUNNY AFTER-NOON, ODIE?
JON'S AWAY. I CAN LIE HERE DOING SOMETHING I ENJOY... WATCHING SOMEONE ELSE EXERCISE.
ONE.
TWO.
ONE.
TWO.
FASTER, YOU FLABBY MICE!
CAN'T WE TAKE A BREAK, BIFF?
LIKE UNTIL NEXT AUGUST?
STOP GOOFING OFF, SQUEAK! NOW DROP AND GIVE ME 20!
YOU COULD GO A LITTLE EASIER ON THEM, BIFF.
BUT, EMILY, THEY HAVE TO BE IN SHAPE TO PROTECT THEMSELVES IN CASE A CAT COMES INTO THE YARD!
YOU MEAN LIKE...
THAT CAT?!
SO MANY TASTY MICE...

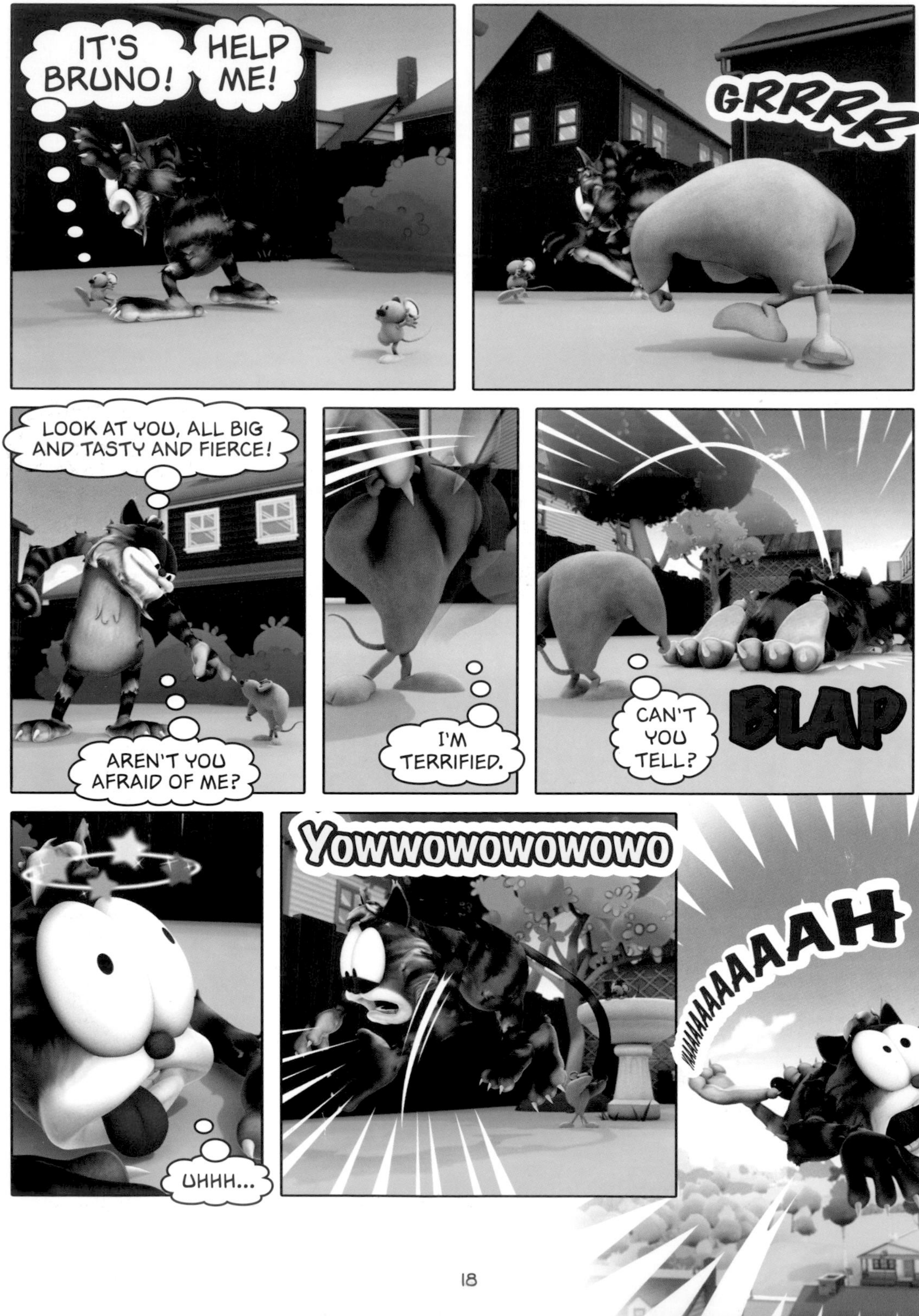
IT'S BRUNO!
HELP ME!
GRRRR
LOOK AT YOU, ALL BIG AND TASTY AND FIERCE!
AREN'T YOU AFRAID OF ME?
I'M TERRIFIED.
CAN'T YOU TELL?
BLAP
UHHH...
YOWWOWOWOWOWO
AAAAAAAAAAAAAAH

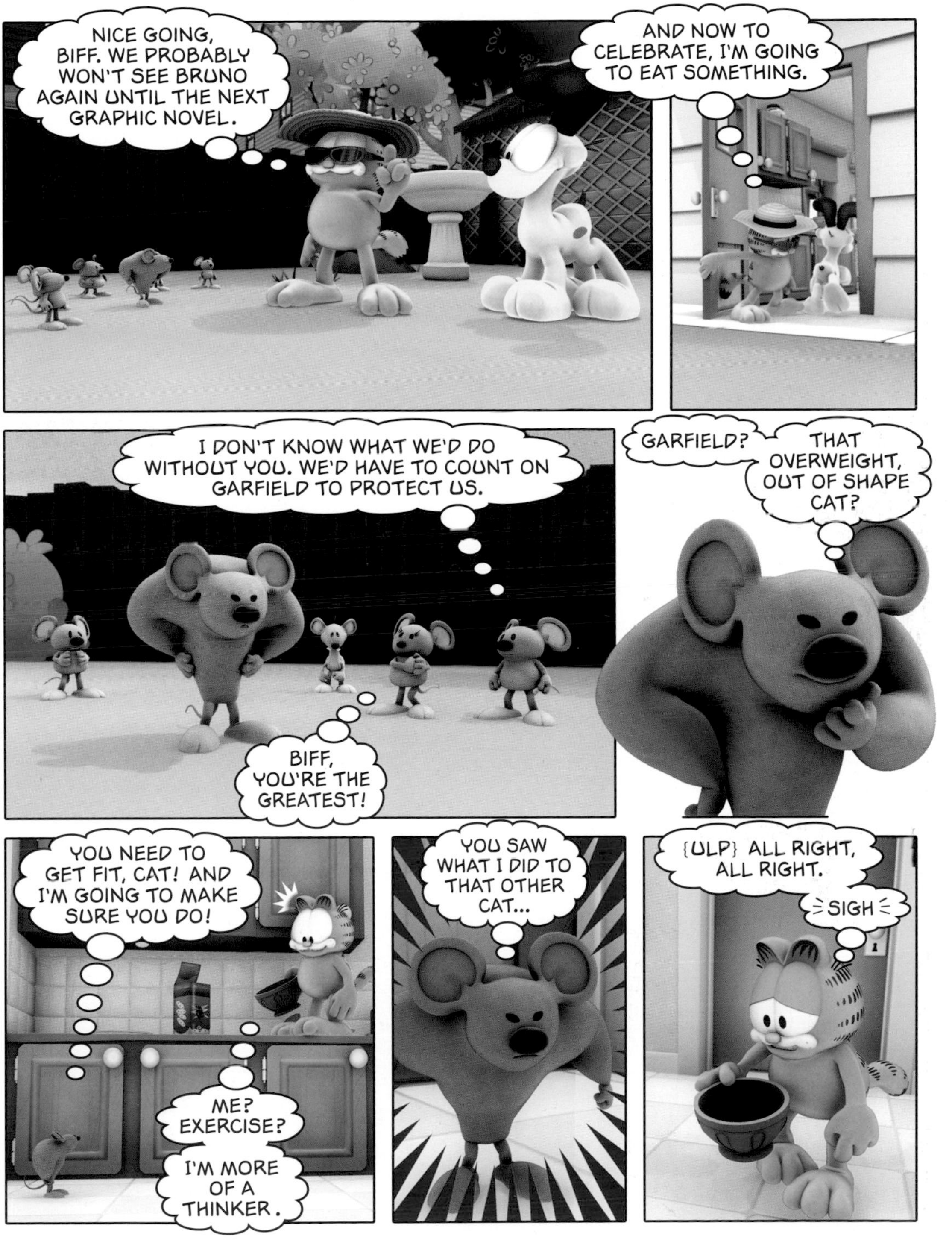
NICE GOING, BIFF. WE PROBABLY WON'T SEE BRUNO AGAIN UNTIL THE NEXT GRAPHIC NOVEL.
AND NOW TO CELEBRATE, I'M GOING TO EAT SOMETHING.
I DON'T KNOW WHAT WE'D DO WITHOUT YOU. WE'D HAVE TO COUNT ON GARFIELD TO PROTECT US.
BIFF, YOU'RE THE GREATEST!
GARFIELD?
THAT OVERWEIGHT, OUT OF SHAPE CAT?
YOU NEED TO GET FIT, CAT! AND I'M GOING TO MAKE SURE YOU DO!
ME? EXERCISE?
I'M MORE OF A THINKER.
YOU SAW WHAT I DID TO THAT OTHER CAT...
{ULP} ALL RIGHT, ALL RIGHT.
SIGH

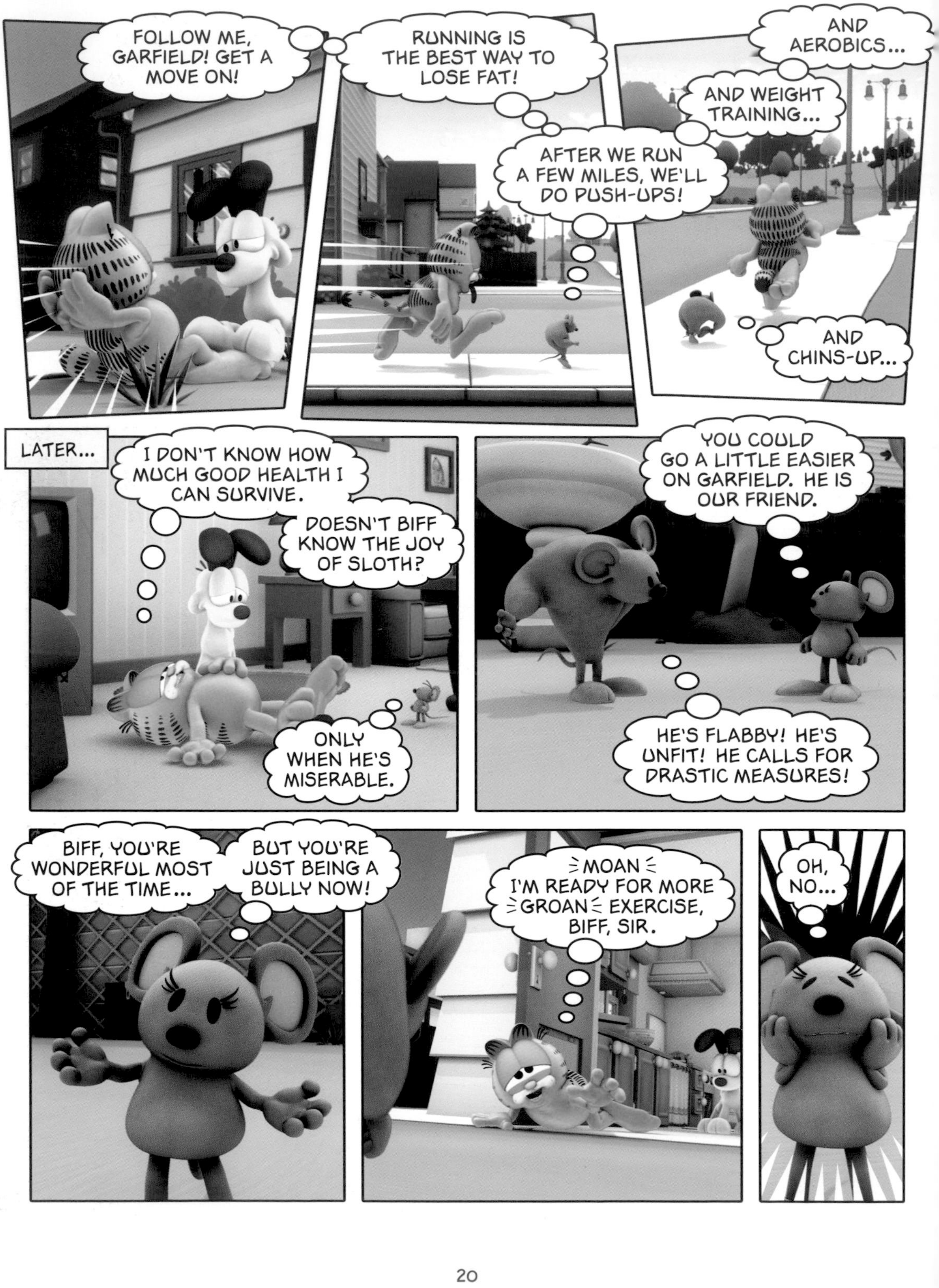
FOLLOW ME, GARFIELD! GET A MOVE ON!
RUNNING IS THE BEST WAY TO LOSE FAT!
AFTER WE RUN A FEW MILES, WE'LL DO PUSH-UPS!
AND WEIGHT TRAINING...
AND AEROBICS...
AND CHINS-UP...
LATER...
I DON'T KNOW HOW MUCH GOOD HEALTH I CAN SURVIVE.
DOESN'T BIFF KNOW THE JOY OF SLOTH?
ONLY WHEN HE'S MISERABLE.
YOU COULD GO A LITTLE EASIER ON GARFIELD. HE IS OUR FRIEND.
HE'S FLABBY! HE'S UNFIT! HE CALLS FOR DRASTIC MEASURES!
BIFF, YOU'RE WONDERFUL MOST OF THE TIME...
BUT YOU'RE JUST BEING A BULLY NOW!
MOAN I'M READY FOR MORE GROAN EXERCISE, BIFF, SIR.
OH, NO...

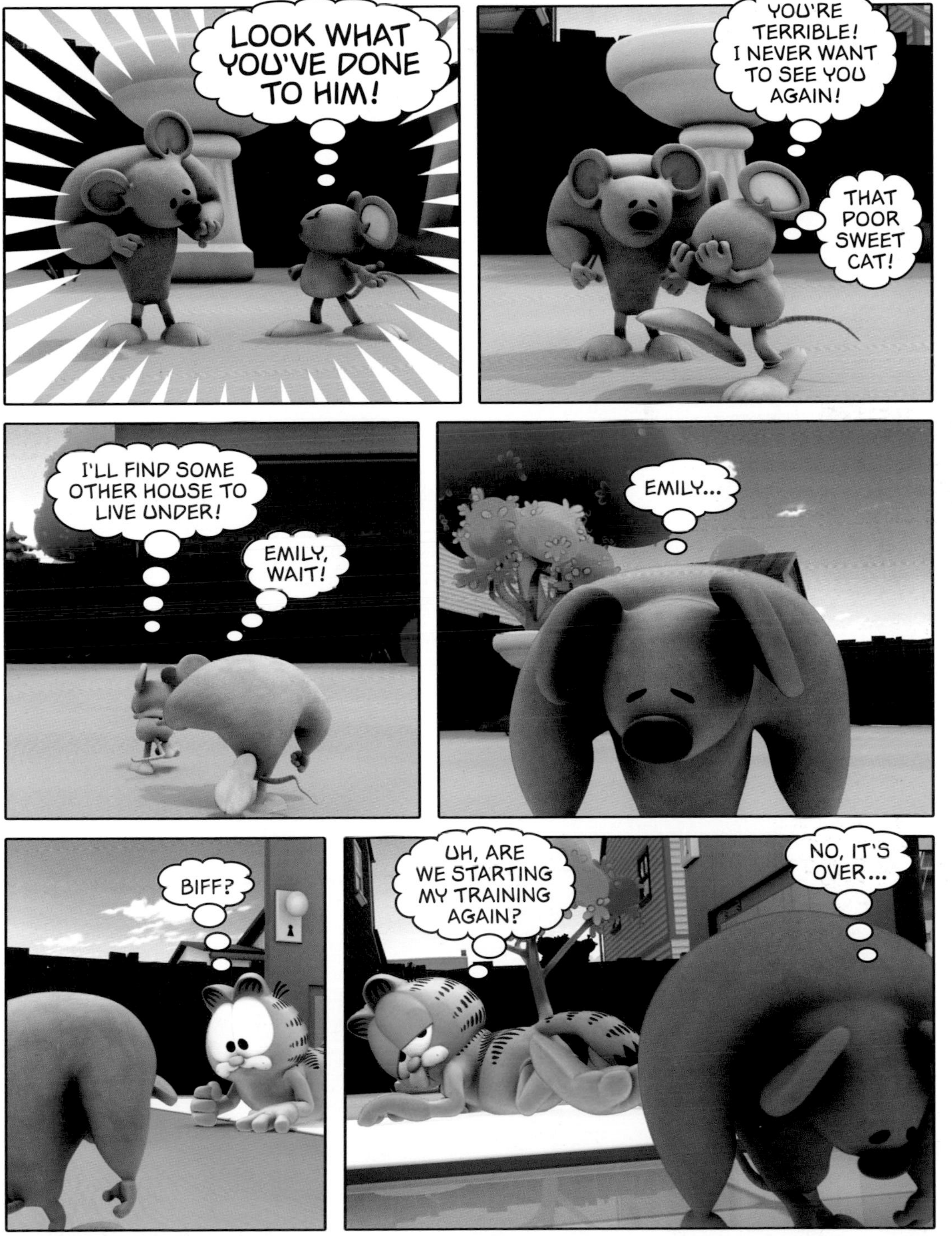
LOOK WHAT YOU'VE DONE TO HIM!
YOU'RE TERRIBLE! I NEVER WANT TO SEE YOU AGAIN!
THAT POOR SWEET CAT!
I'LL FIND SOME OTHER HOUSE TO LIVE UNDER!
EMILY, WAIT!
EMILY...
BIFF?
UH, ARE WE STARTING MY TRAINING AGAIN?
NO, IT'S OVER...

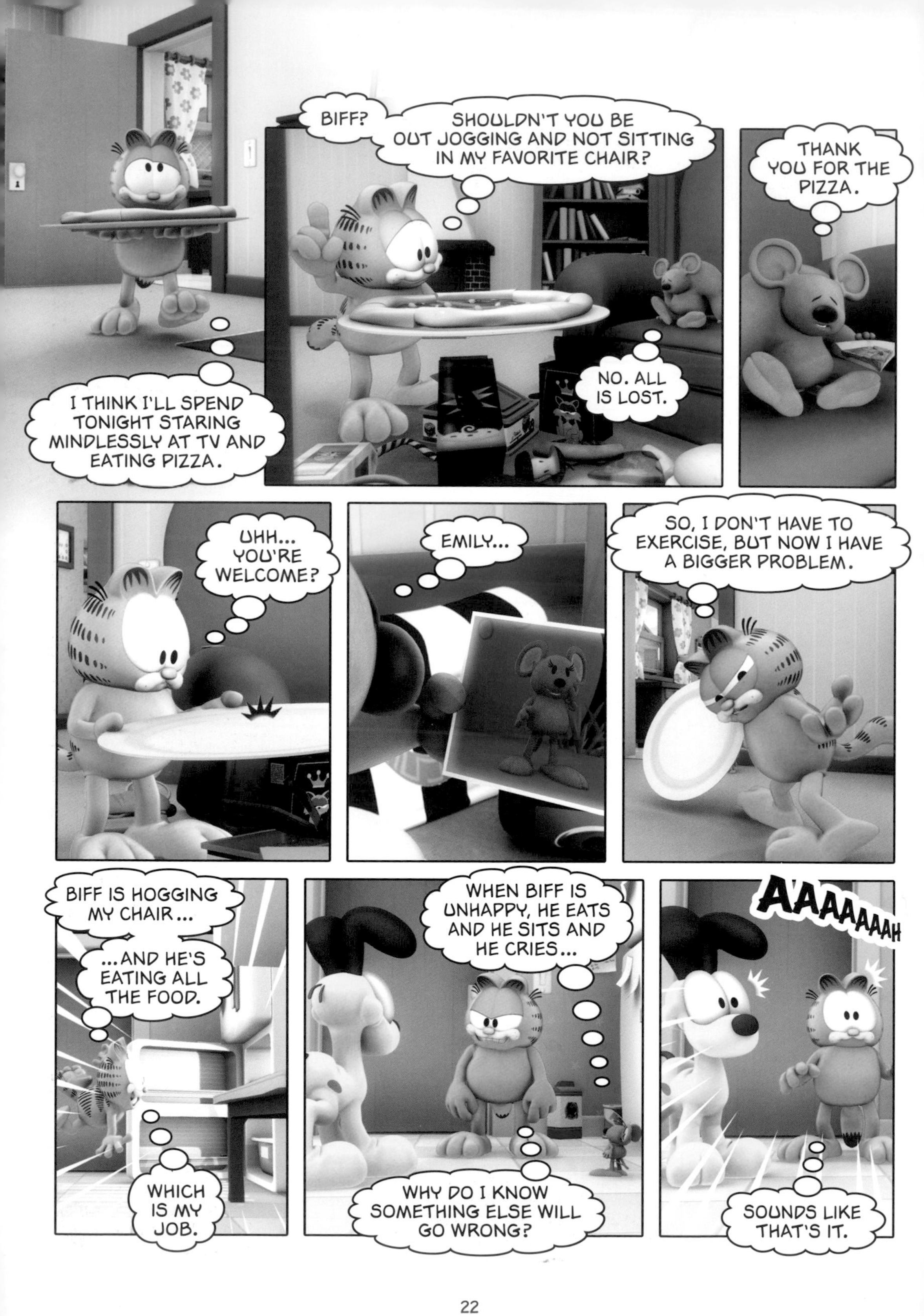

I THINK I'LL SPEND TONIGHT STARING MINDLESSLY AT TV AND EATING PIZZA.
BIFF?
SHOULDN'T YOU BE OUT JOGGING AND NOT SITTING IN MY FAVORITE CHAIR?
NO. ALL IS LOST.
THANK YOU FOR THE PIZZA.
UHH... YOU'RE WELCOME?
EMILY...
SO, I DON'T HAVE TO EXERCISE, BUT NOW I HAVE A BIGGER PROBLEM.
BIFF IS HOGGING MY CHAIR...
...AND HE'S EATING ALL THE FOOD.
WHICH IS MY JOB.
WHEN BIFF IS UNHAPPY, HE EATS AND HE SITS AND HE CRIES...
WHY DO I KNOW SOMETHING ELSE WILL GO WRONG?
AAAAAAAH
SOUNDS LIKE THAT'S IT.

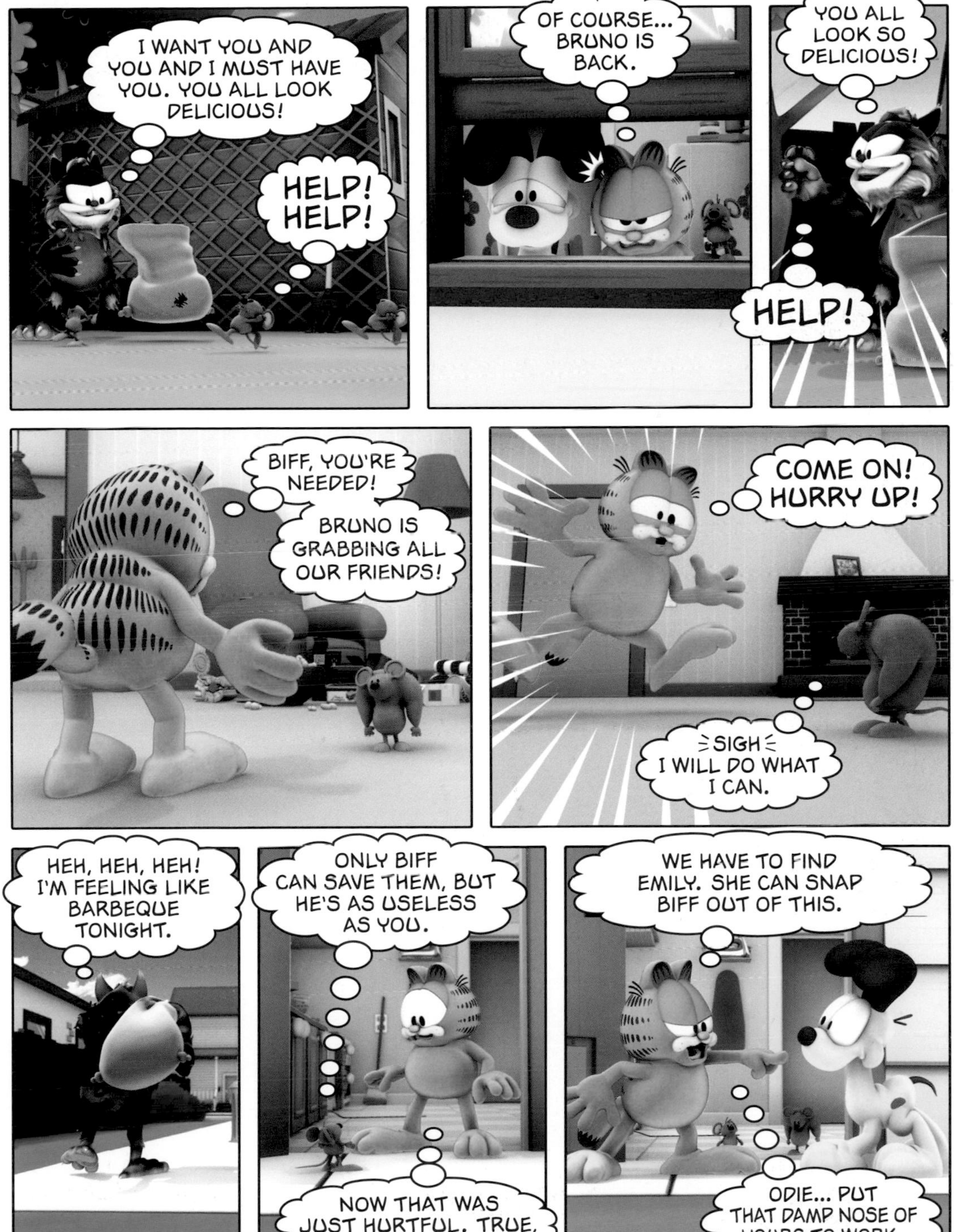
I WANT YOU AND YOU AND I MUST HAVE YOU. YOU ALL LOOK DELICIOUS!
HELP! HELP!
OF COURSE... BRUNO IS BACK.
YOU ALL LOOK SO DELICIOUS!
HELP!
BIFF, YOU'RE NEEDED!
BRUNO IS GRABBING ALL OUR FRIENDS!
COME ON! HURRY UP!
SIGH I WILL DO WHAT I CAN.
HEH, HEH, HEH! I'M FEELING LIKE BARBEQUE TONIGHT.
ONLY BIFF CAN SAVE THEM, BUT HE'S AS USELESS AS YOU.
NOW THAT WAS JUST HURTFUL. TRUE, BUT HURTFUL.
WE HAVE TO FIND EMILY. SHE CAN SNAP BIFF OUT OF THIS.
ODIE... PUT THAT DAMP NOSE OF YOURS TO WORK.

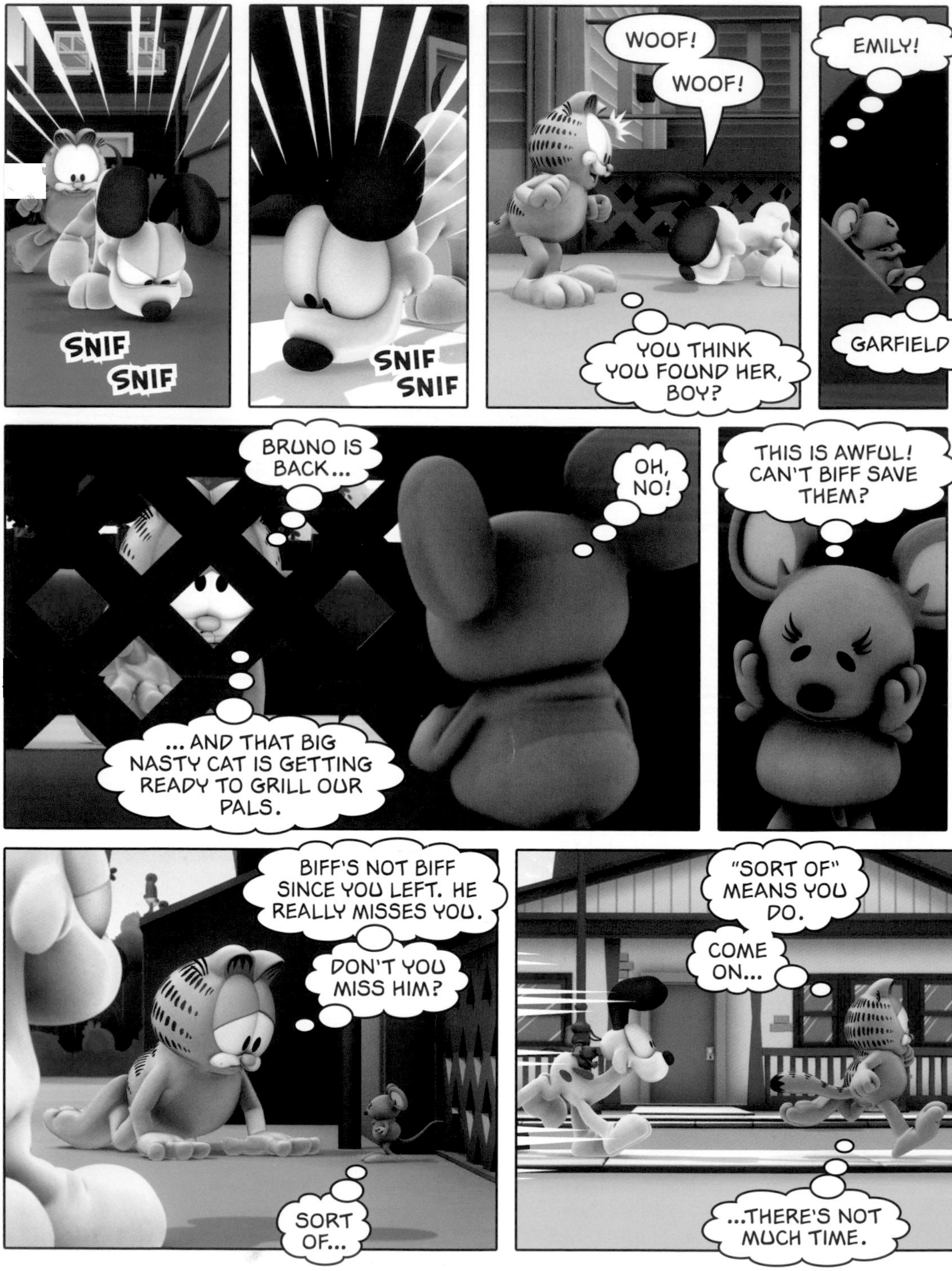
SNIF
SNIF
SNIF
SNIF
WOOF!
WOOF!
YOU THINK YOU FOUND HER, BOY?
EMILY!
GARFIELD?
BRUNO IS BACK...
... AND THAT BIG NASTY CAT IS GETTING READY TO GRILL OUR PALS.
OH, NO!
THIS IS AWFUL! CAN'T BIFF SAVE THEM?
BIFF'S NOT BIFF SINCE YOU LEFT. HE REALLY MISSES YOU.
DON'T YOU MISS HIM?
SORT OF...
"SORT OF" MEANS YOU DO.
COME ON...
...THERE'S NOT MUCH TIME.

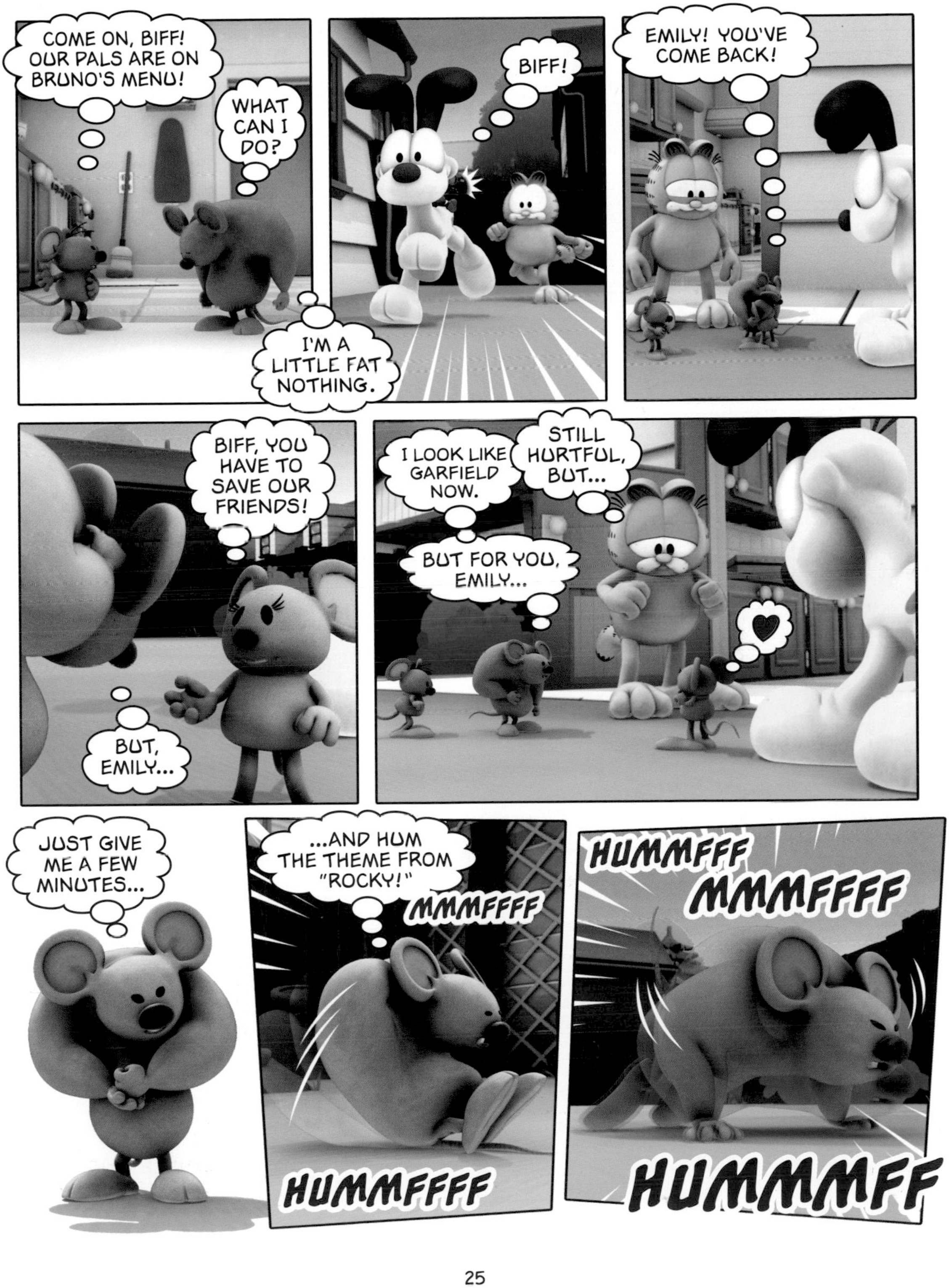
COME ON, BIFF! OUR PALS ARE ON BRUNO'S MENU!
WHAT CAN I DO?
I'M A LITTLE FAT NOTHING.
BIFF!
EMILY! YOU'VE COME BACK!
BIFF, YOU HAVE TO SAVE OUR FRIENDS!
BUT, EMILY...
I LOOK LIKE GARFIELD NOW.
STILL HURTFUL, BUT...
BUT FOR YOU, EMILY...
JUST GIVE ME A FEW MINUTES...
...AND HUM THE THEME FROM "ROCKY!"
MMMFFFF
HUMMFFFF
HUMMFFF
MMMFFFF
HUMMMFF

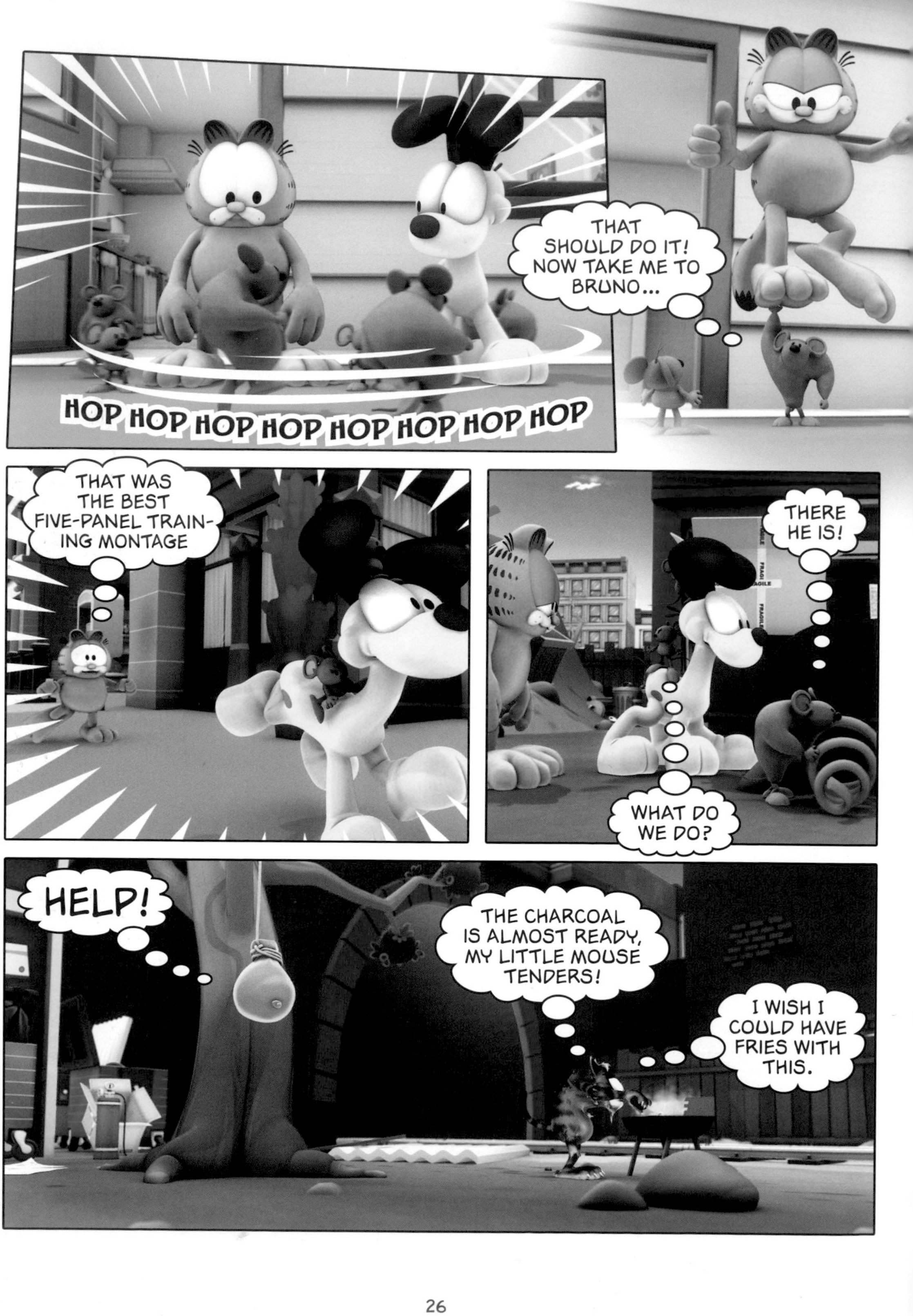
THAT SHOULD DO IT! NOW TAKE ME TO BRUNO...
HOP HOP HOP HOP HOP HOP HOP HOP
THAT WAS THE BEST FIVE-PANEL TRAINING MONTAGE
THERE HE IS!
WHAT DO WE DO?
HELP!
THE CHARCOAL IS ALMOST READY, MY LITTLE MOUSE TENDERS!
I WISH I COULD HAVE FRIES WITH THIS.

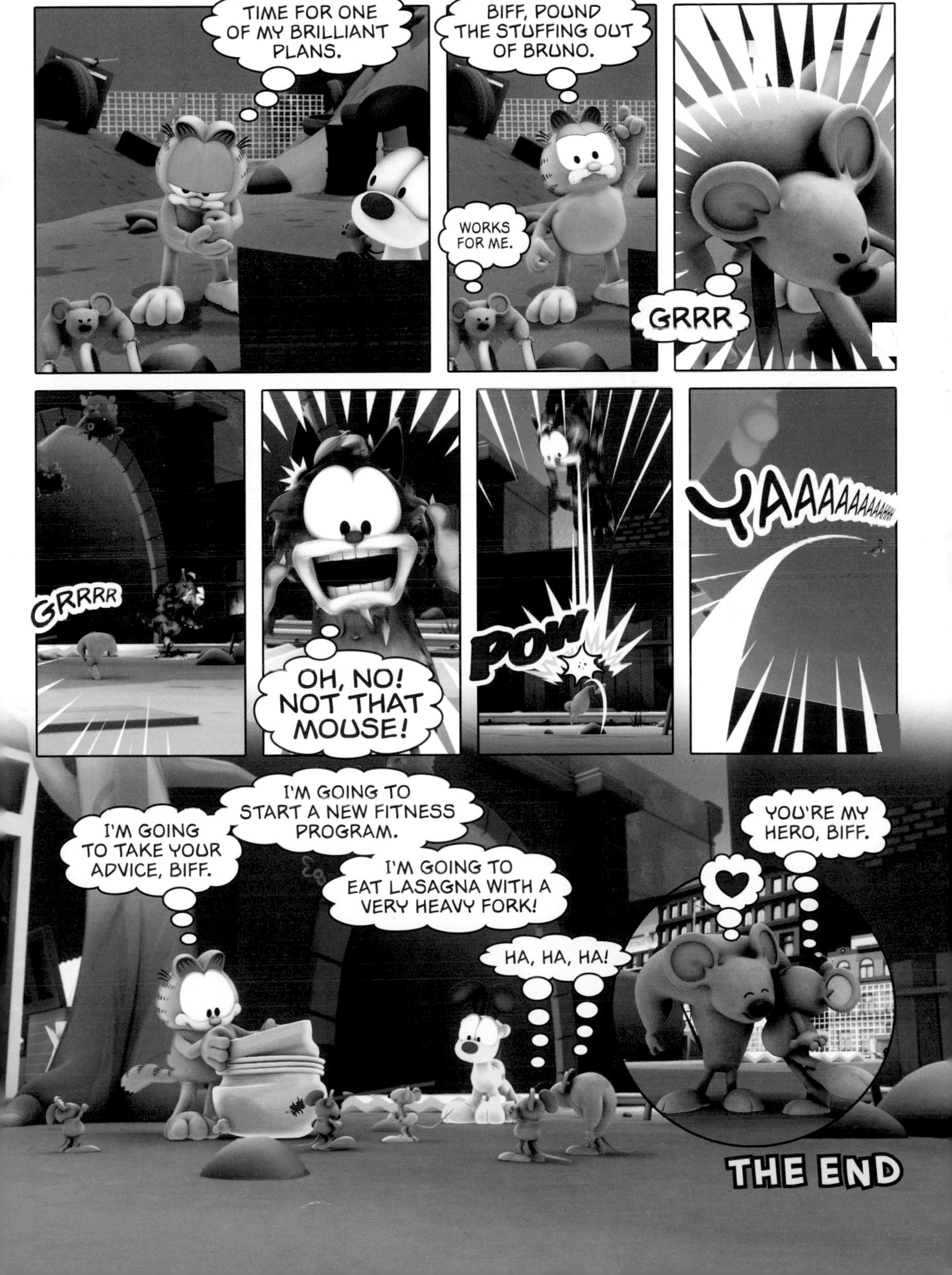
TIME FOR ONE OF MY BRILLIANT PLANS.
BIFF, POUND THE STUFFING OUT OF BRUNO.
WORKS FOR ME.
GRRR
GRRRR
OH, NO! NOT THAT MOUSE!
POW
YAAAAAAAAAHH
I'M GOING TO TAKE YOUR ADVICE, BIFF.
I'M GOING TO START A NEW FITNESS PROGRAM.
I'M GOING TO EAT LASAGNA WITH A VERY HEAVY FORK!
HA, HA, HA!
YOU'RE MY HERO, BIFF.
THE END

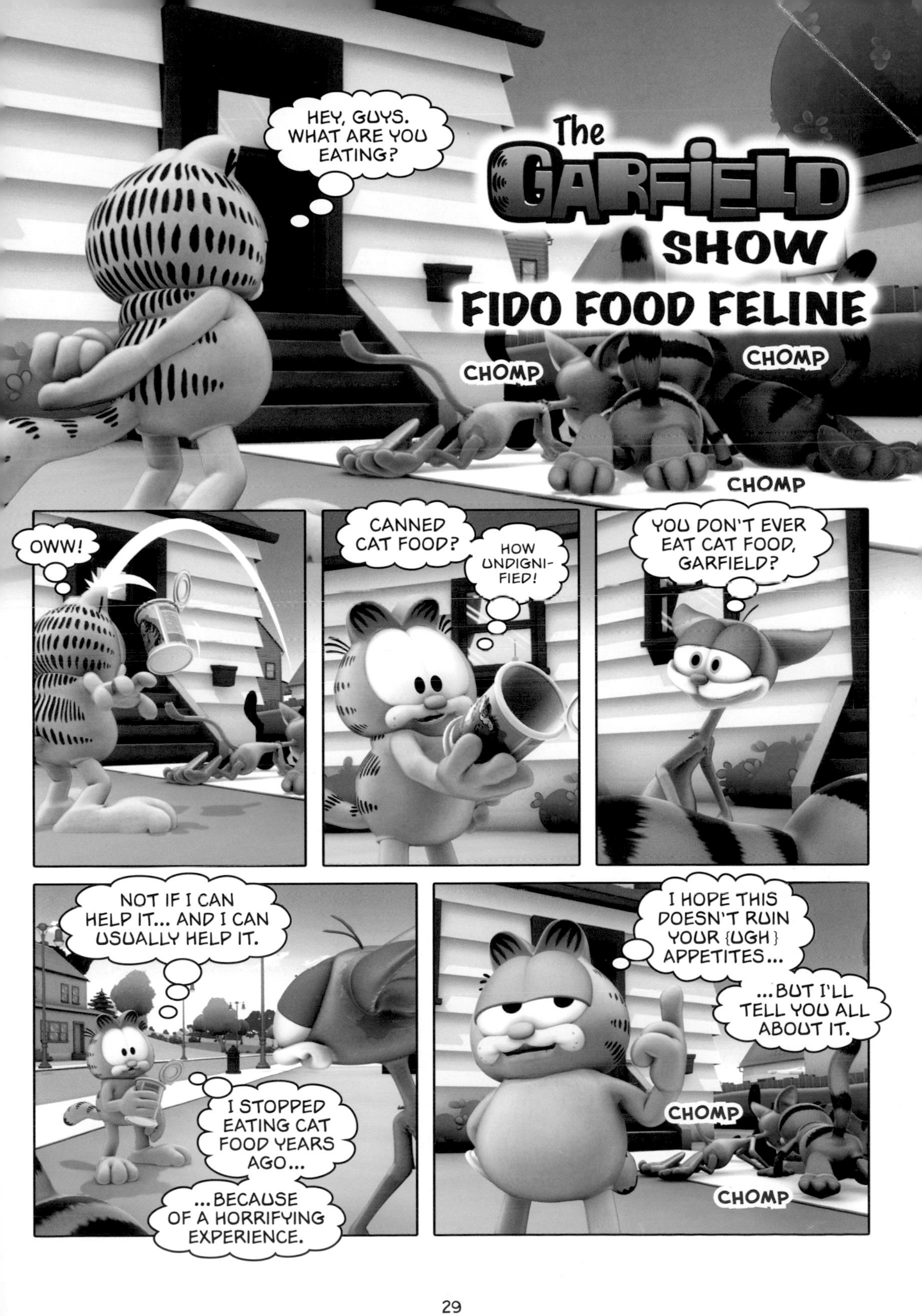
HEY, GUYS. WHAT ARE YOU EATING?
The GARFIELD SHOW
FIDO FOOD FELINE
CHOMP
CHOMP
CHOMP
OWW!
CANNED CAT FOOD?
HOW UNDIGNI-FIED!
YOU DON'T EVER EAT CAT FOOD, GARFIELD?
NOT IF I CAN HELP IT... AND I CAN USUALLY HELP IT.
I STOPPED EATING CAT FOOD YEARS AGO...
...BECAUSE OF A HORRIFYING EXPERIENCE.
I HOPE THIS DOESN'T RUIN YOUR {UGH} APPETITES...
...BUT I'LL TELL YOU ALL ABOUT IT.
CHOMP
CHOMP

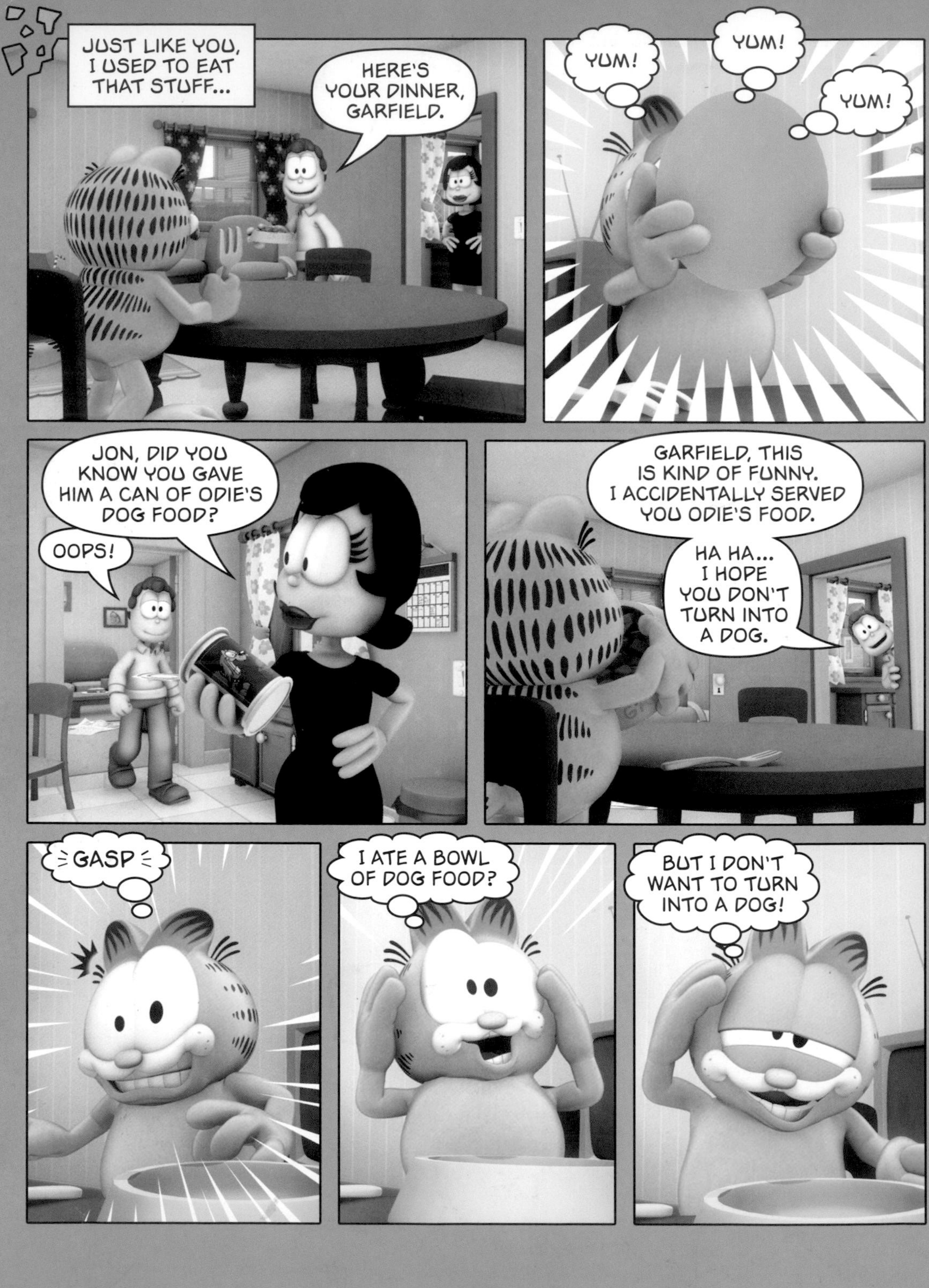
JUST LIKE YOU, I USED TO EAT THAT STUFF...
HERE'S YOUR DINNER, GARFIELD.
YUM!
YUM!
YUM!
JON, DID YOU KNOW YOU GAVE HIM A CAN OF ODIE'S DOG FOOD?
OOPS!
GARFIELD, THIS IS KIND OF FUNNY. I ACCIDENTALLY SERVED YOU ODIE'S FOOD.
HA HA... I HOPE YOU DON'T TURN INTO A DOG.
GASP
I ATE A BOWL OF DOG FOOD?
BUT I DON'T WANT TO TURN INTO A DOG!

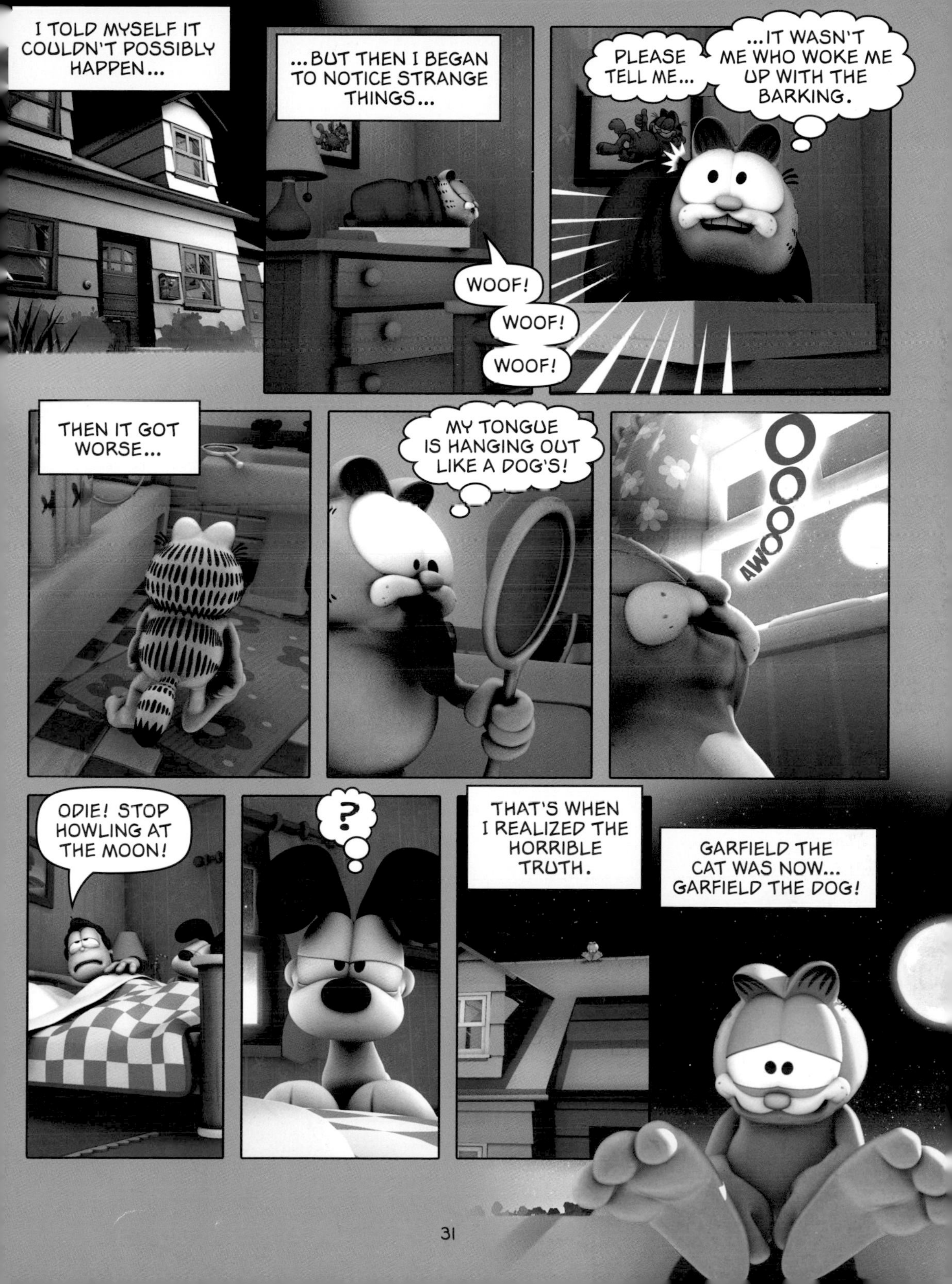
I TOLD MYSELF IT COULDN'T POSSIBLY HAPPEN...
...BUT THEN I BEGAN TO NOTICE STRANGE THINGS...
WOOF!
WOOF!
WOOF!
PLEASE TELL ME...
...IT WASN'T ME WHO WOKE ME UP WITH THE BARKING.
THEN IT GOT WORSE...
MY TONGUE IS HANGING OUT LIKE A DOG'S!
AWOOOO
ODIE! STOP HOWLING AT THE MOON!
?
THAT'S WHEN I REALIZED THE HORRIBLE TRUTH.
GARFIELD THE CAT WAS NOW... GARFIELD THE DOG!

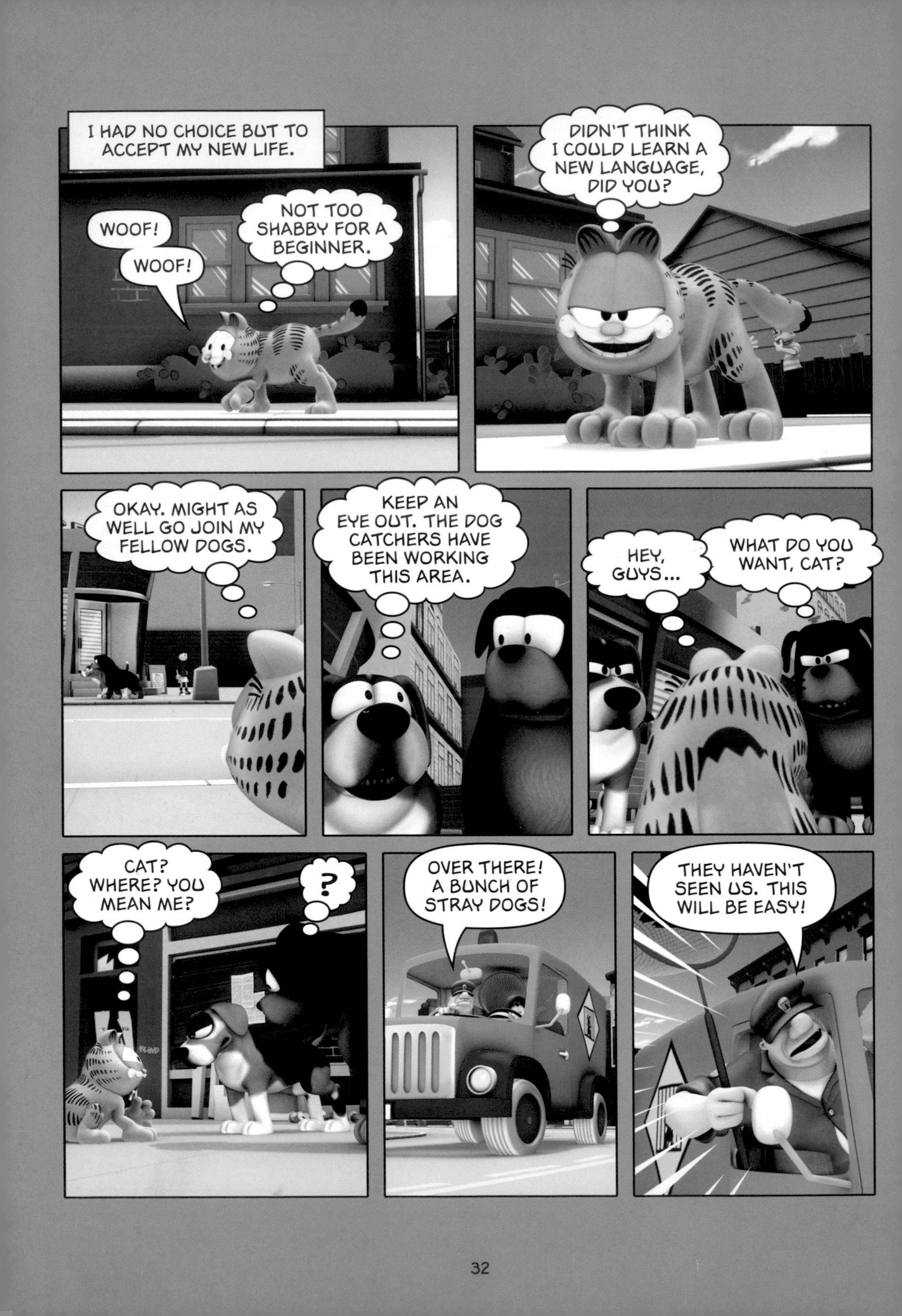
I HAD NO CHOICE BUT TO ACCEPT MY NEW LIFE.
WOOF!
WOOF!
NOT TOO SHABBY FOR A BEGINNER.
DIDN'T THINK I COULD LEARN A NEW LANGUAGE, DID YOU?
OKAY. MIGHT AS WELL GO JOIN MY FELLOW DOGS.
KEEP AN EYE OUT. THE DOG CATCHERS HAVE BEEN WORKING THIS AREA.
HEY, GUYS...
WHAT DO YOU WANT, CAT?
CAT? WHERE? YOU MEAN ME?
?
OVER THERE! A BUNCH OF STRAY DOGS!
THEY HAVEN'T SEEN US. THIS WILL BE EASY!

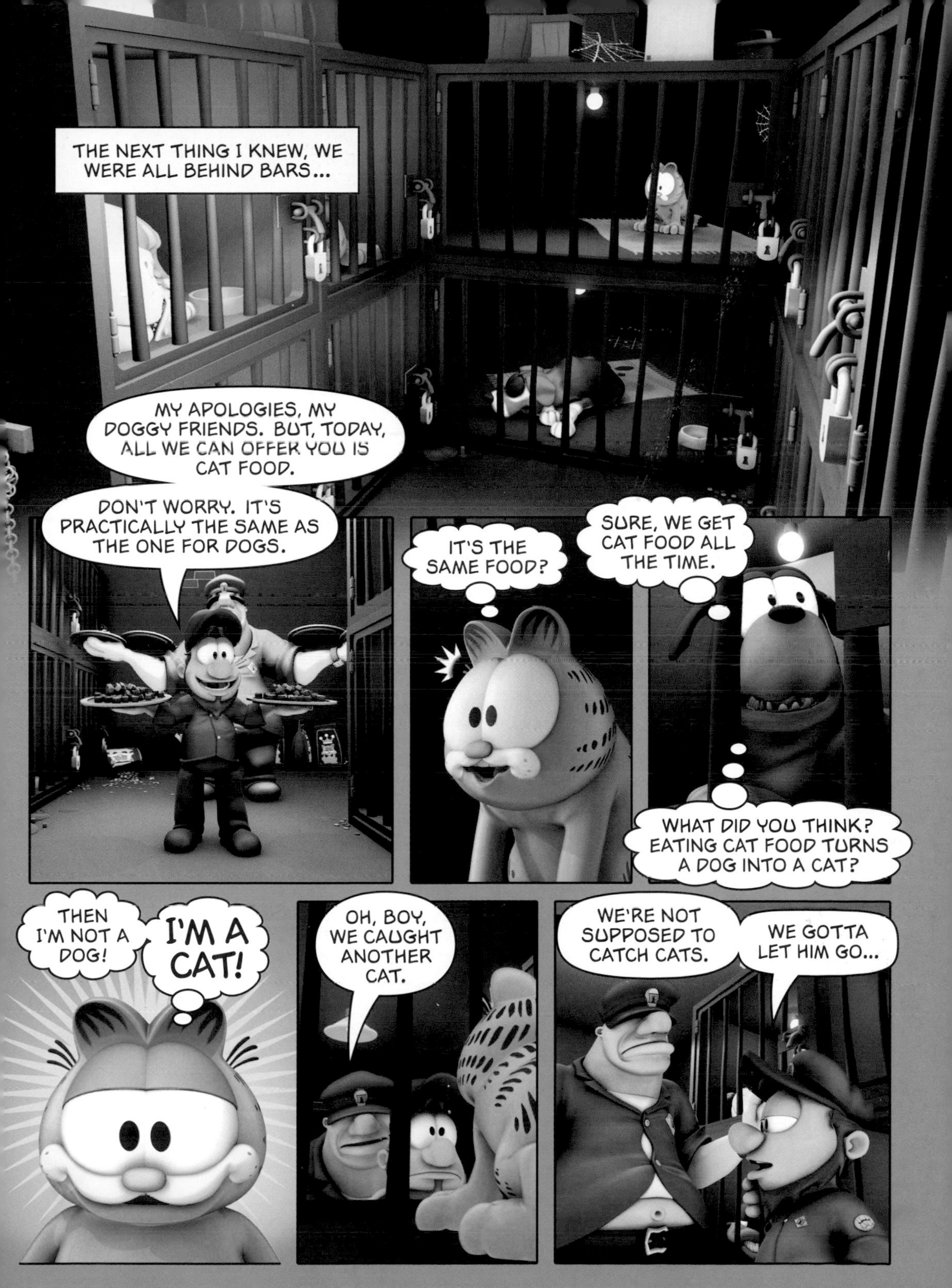
THE NEXT THING I KNEW, WE WERE ALL BEHIND BARS...
MY APOLOGIES, MY DOGGY FRIENDS. BUT, TODAY, ALL WE CAN OFFER YOU IS CAT FOOD.
DON'T WORRY. IT'S PRACTICALLY THE SAME AS THE ONE FOR DOGS.
IT'S THE SAME FOOD?
SURE, WE GET CAT FOOD ALL THE TIME.
WHAT DID YOU THINK? EATING CAT FOOD TURNS A DOG INTO A CAT?
THEN I'M NOT A DOG!
I'M A CAT!
OH, BOY, WE CAUGHT ANOTHER CAT.
WE'RE NOT SUPPOSED TO CATCH CATS.
WE GOTTA LET HIM GO...

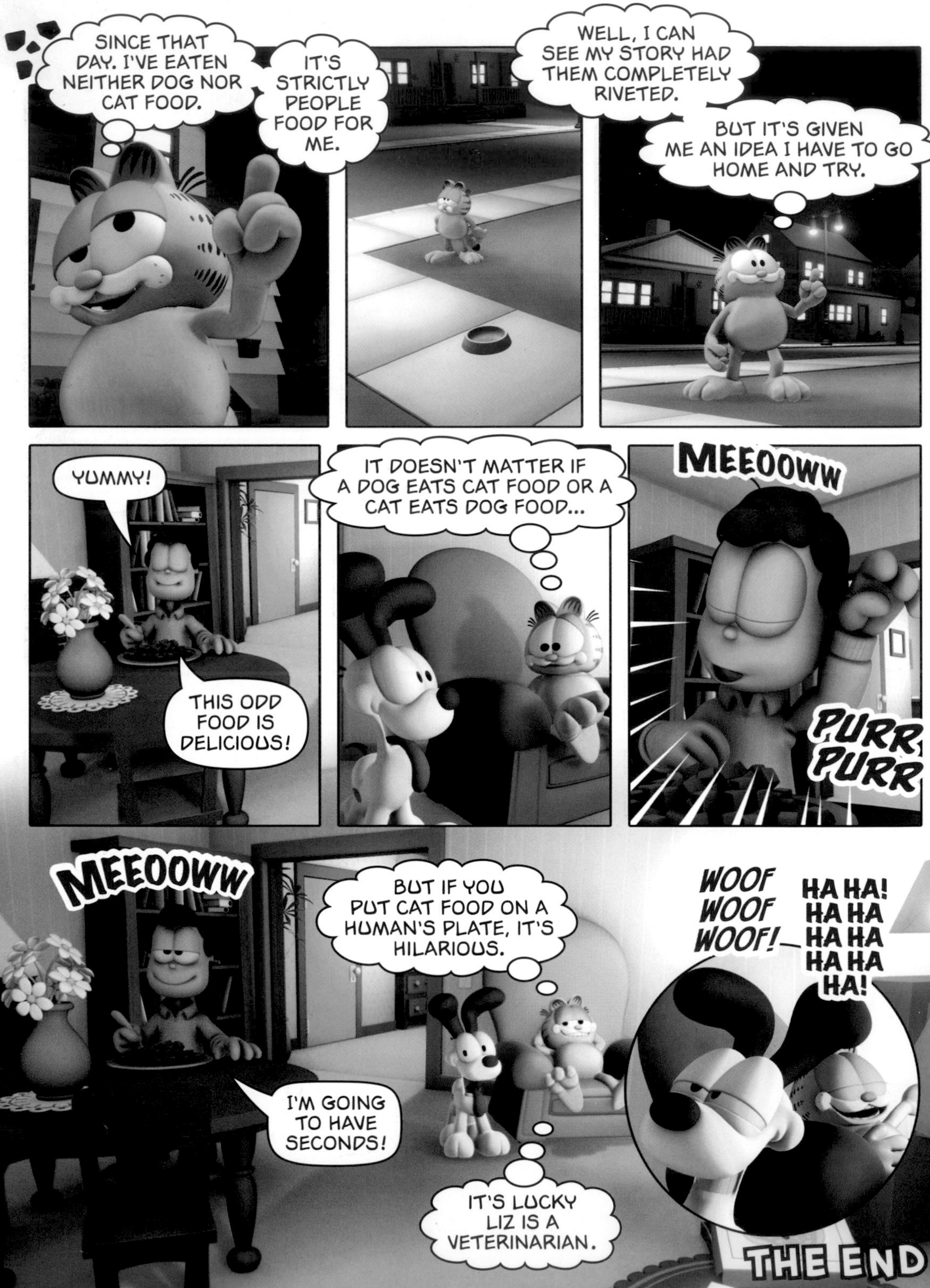

SINCE THAT DAY. I'VE EATEN NEITHER DOG NOR CAT FOOD.
IT'S STRICTLY PEOPLE FOOD FOR ME.
WELL, I CAN SEE MY STORY HAD THEM COMPLETELY RIVETED.
BUT IT'S GIVEN ME AN IDEA I HAVE TO GO HOME AND TRY.
YUMMY!
THIS ODD FOOD IS DELICIOUS!
IT DOESN'T MATTER IF A DOG EATS CAT FOOD OR A CAT EATS DOG FOOD...
MEEOOWW
PURR PURR
MEEOOWW
BUT IF YOU PUT CAT FOOD ON A HUMAN'S PLATE, IT'S HILARIOUS.
I'M GOING TO HAVE SECONDS!
IT'S LUCKY LIZ IS A VETERINARIAN.
WOOF WOOF WOOF!
HA HA! HA HA HA HA HA HA HA!
THE END

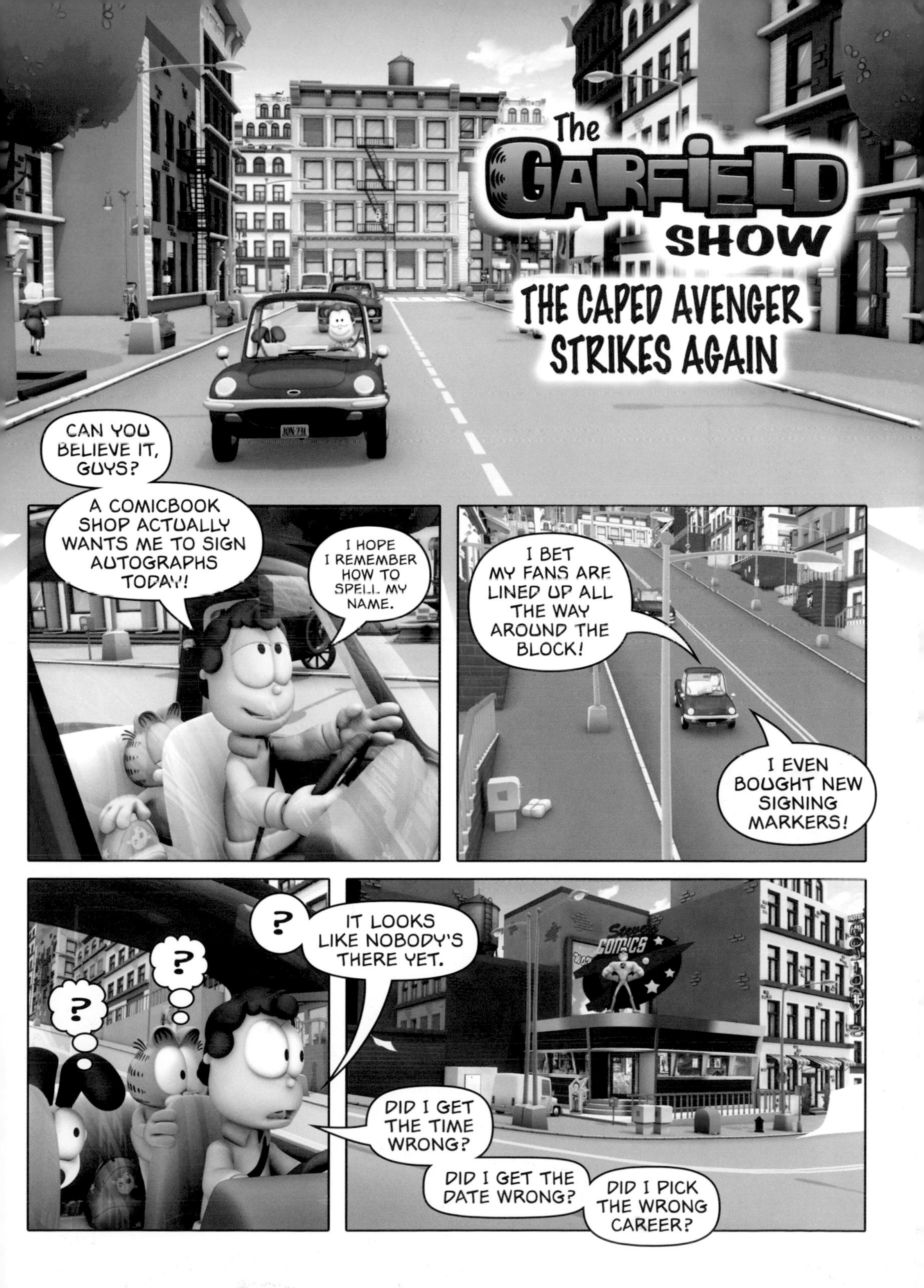
The GARFIELD SHOW
THE CAPED AVENGER STRIKES AGAIN
CAN YOU BELIEVE IT, GUYS?
A COMICBOOK SHOP ACTUALLY WANTS ME TO SIGN AUTOGRAPHS TODAY!
I HOPE I REMEMBER HOW TO SPELL MY NAME.
I BET MY FANS ARE LINED UP ALL THE WAY AROUND THE BLOCK!
I EVEN BOUGHT NEW SIGNING MARKERS!
?
?
?
IT LOOKS LIKE NOBODY'S THERE YET.
COMICS
DID I GET THE TIME WRONG?
DID I GET THE DATE WRONG?
DID I PICK THE WRONG CAREER?

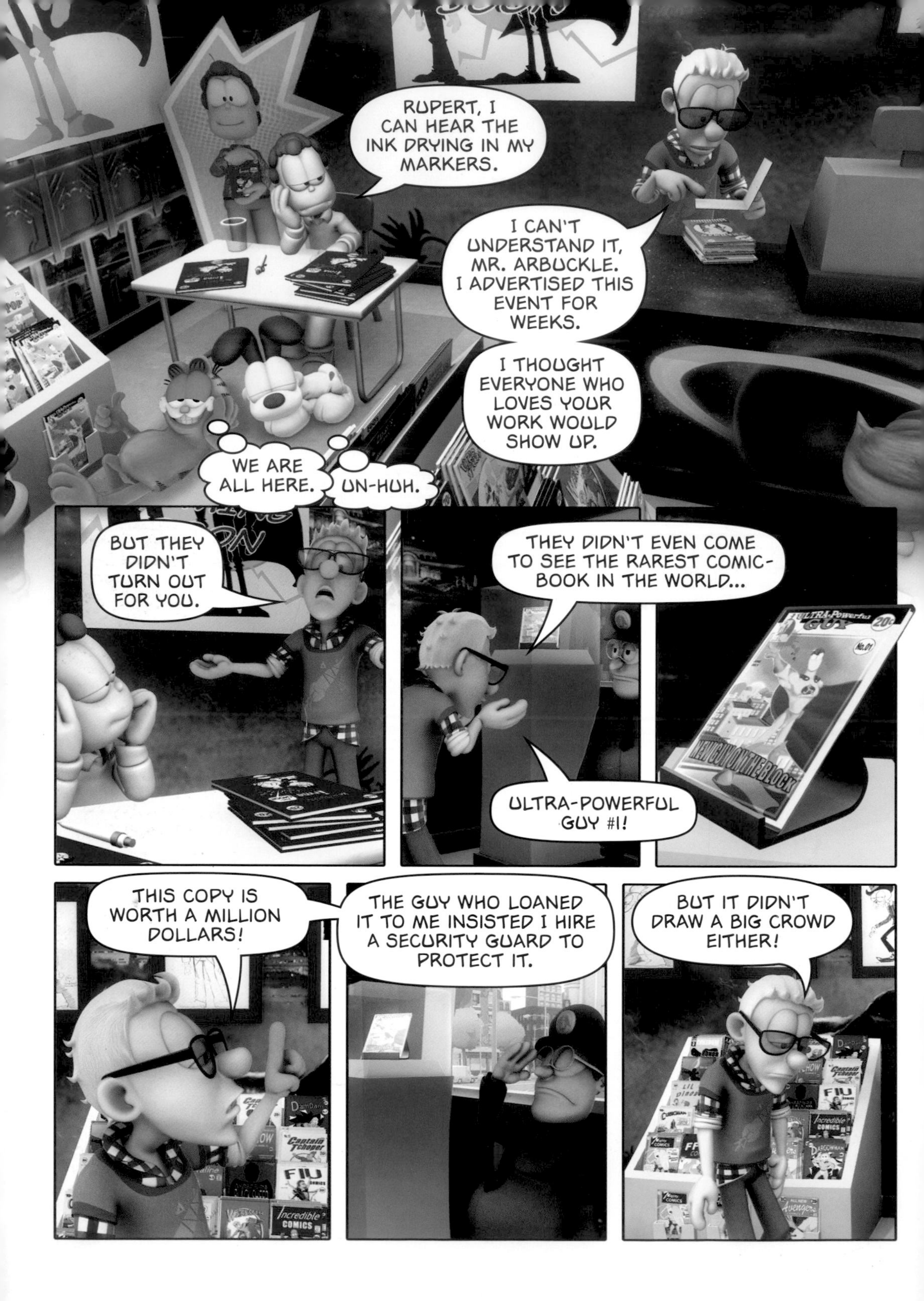
RUPERT, I CAN HEAR THE INK DRYING IN MY MARKERS.
I CAN'T UNDERSTAND IT, MR. ARBUCKLE. I ADVERTISED THIS EVENT FOR WEEKS.
I THOUGHT EVERYONE WHO LOVES YOUR WORK WOULD SHOW UP.
WE ARE ALL HERE.
UN-HUH.
BUT THEY DIDN'T TURN OUT FOR YOU.
THEY DIDN'T EVEN COME TO SEE THE RAREST COMIC-BOOK IN THE WORLD...
ULTRA-POWERFUL GUY #1!
THIS COPY IS WORTH A MILLION DOLLARS!
THE GUY WHO LOANED IT TO ME INSISTED I HIRE A SECURITY GUARD TO PROTECT IT.
BUT IT DIDN'T DRAW A BIG CROWD EITHER!

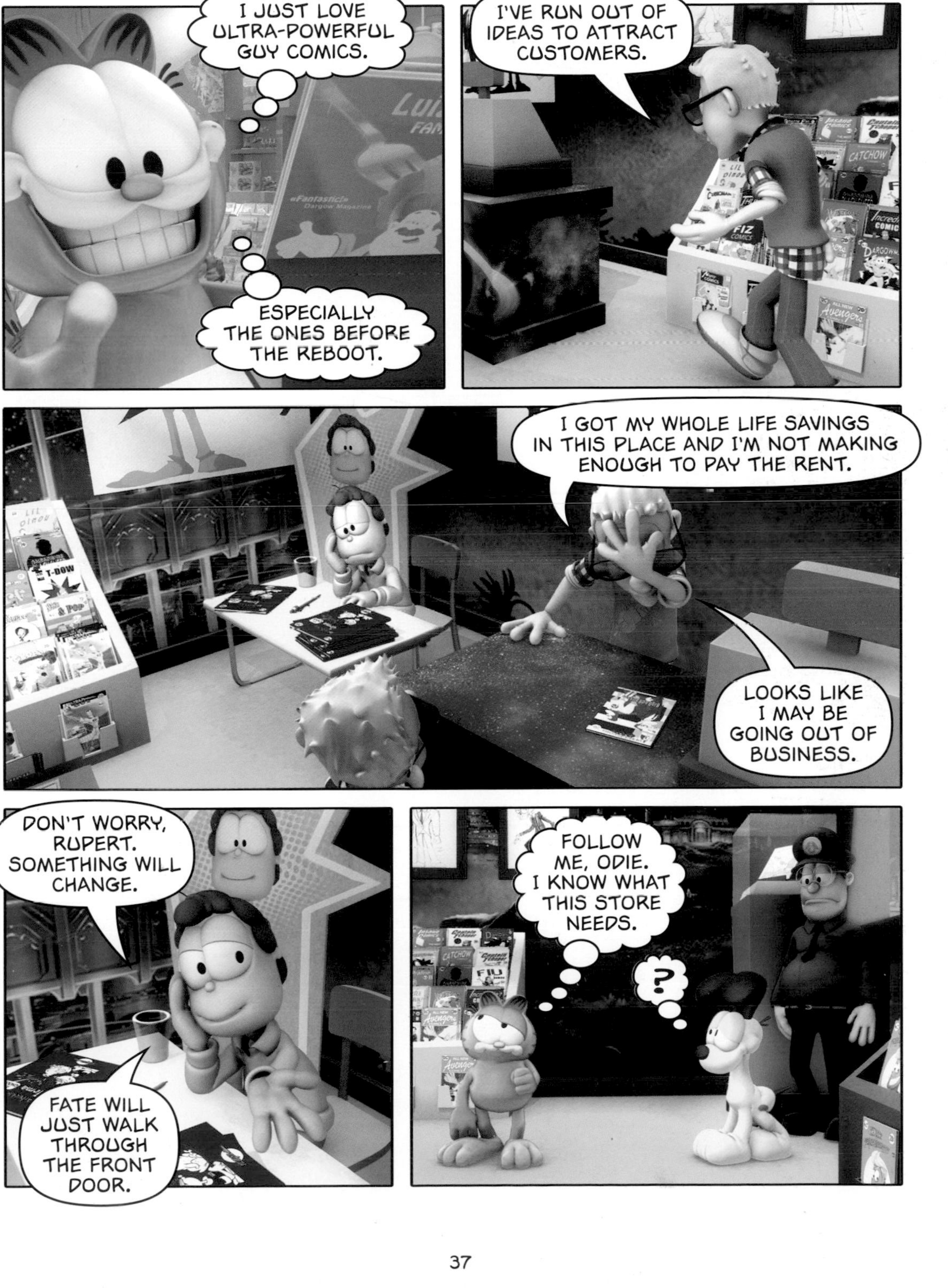

I JUST LOVE ULTRA-POWERFUL GUY COMICS.
ESPECIALLY THE ONES BEFORE THE REBOOT.
I'VE RUN OUT OF IDEAS TO ATTRACT CUSTOMERS.
I GOT MY WHOLE LIFE SAVINGS IN THIS PLACE AND I'M NOT MAKING ENOUGH TO PAY THE RENT.
LOOKS LIKE I MAY BE GOING OUT OF BUSINESS.
DON'T WORRY, RUPERT. SOMETHING WILL CHANGE.
FATE WILL JUST WALK THROUGH THE FRONT DOOR.
FOLLOW ME, ODIE. I KNOW WHAT THIS STORE NEEDS.
?

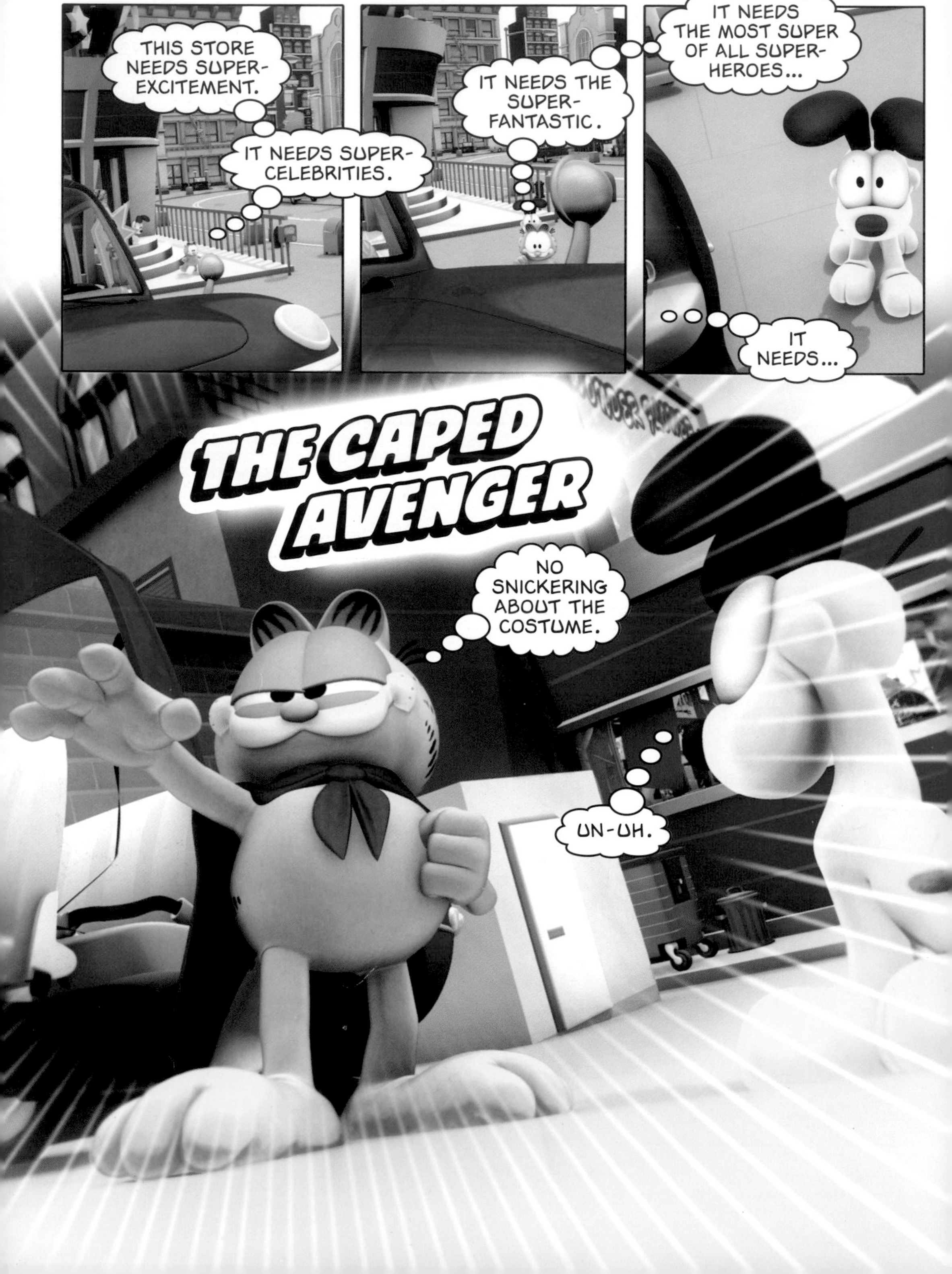
THIS STORE NEEDS SUPER-EXCITEMENT.
IT NEEDS SUPER-CELEBRITIES.
IT NEEDS THE SUPER-FANTASTIC.
IT NEEDS THE MOST SUPER OF ALL SUPER-HEROES...
IT NEEDS...
THE CAPED AVENGER
NO SNICKERING ABOUT THE COSTUME.
UN-UH.

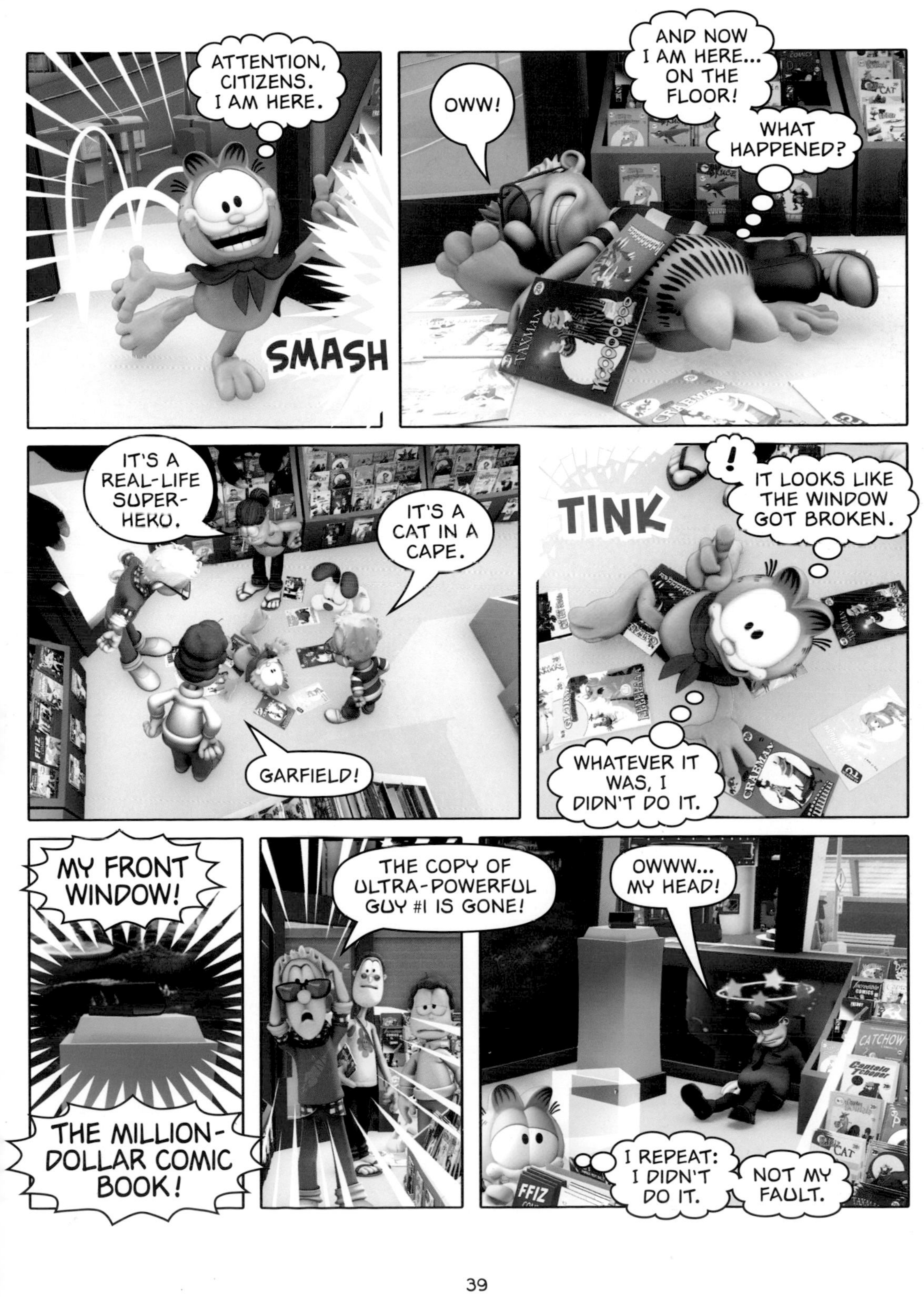

ATTENTION, CITIZENS. I AM HERE.
SMASH
OWW!
AND NOW I AM HERE... ON THE FLOOR!
WHAT HAPPENED?
IT'S A REAL-LIFE SUPER-HERO.
IT'S A CAT IN A CAPE.
GARFIELD!
TINK
!
IT LOOKS LIKE THE WINDOW GOT BROKEN.
WHATEVER IT WAS, I DIDN'T DO IT.
MY FRONT WINDOW!
THE MILLION-DOLLAR COMIC BOOK!
THE COPY OF ULTRA-POWERFUL GUY #1 IS GONE!
OWWW... MY HEAD!
I REPEAT: I DIDN'T DO IT.
NOT MY FAULT.

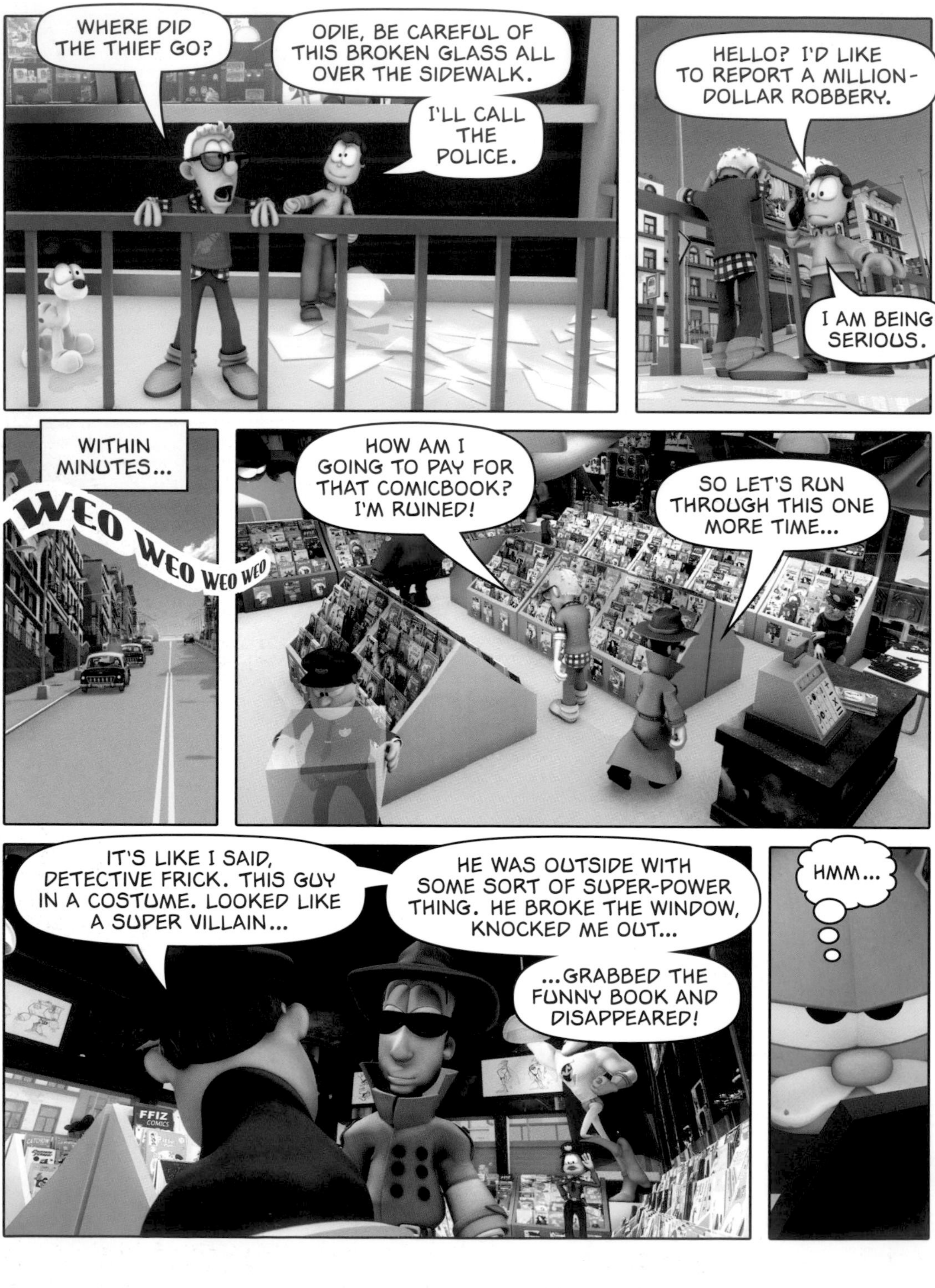
WHERE DID THE THIEF GO?
ODIE, BE CAREFUL OF THIS BROKEN GLASS ALL OVER THE SIDEWALK.
I'LL CALL THE POLICE.
HELLO? I'D LIKE TO REPORT A MILLION-DOLLAR ROBBERY.
I AM BEING SERIOUS.
WITHIN MINUTES...
WEO WEO WEO WEO
HOW AM I GOING TO PAY FOR THAT COMICBOOK? I'M RUINED!
SO LET'S RUN THROUGH THIS ONE MORE TIME...
IT'S LIKE I SAID, DETECTIVE FRICK. THIS GUY IN A COSTUME. LOOKED LIKE A SUPER VILLAIN...
HE WAS OUTSIDE WITH SOME SORT OF SUPER-POWER THING. HE BROKE THE WINDOW, KNOCKED ME OUT...
...GRABBED THE FUNNY BOOK AND DISAPPEARED!
HMM...

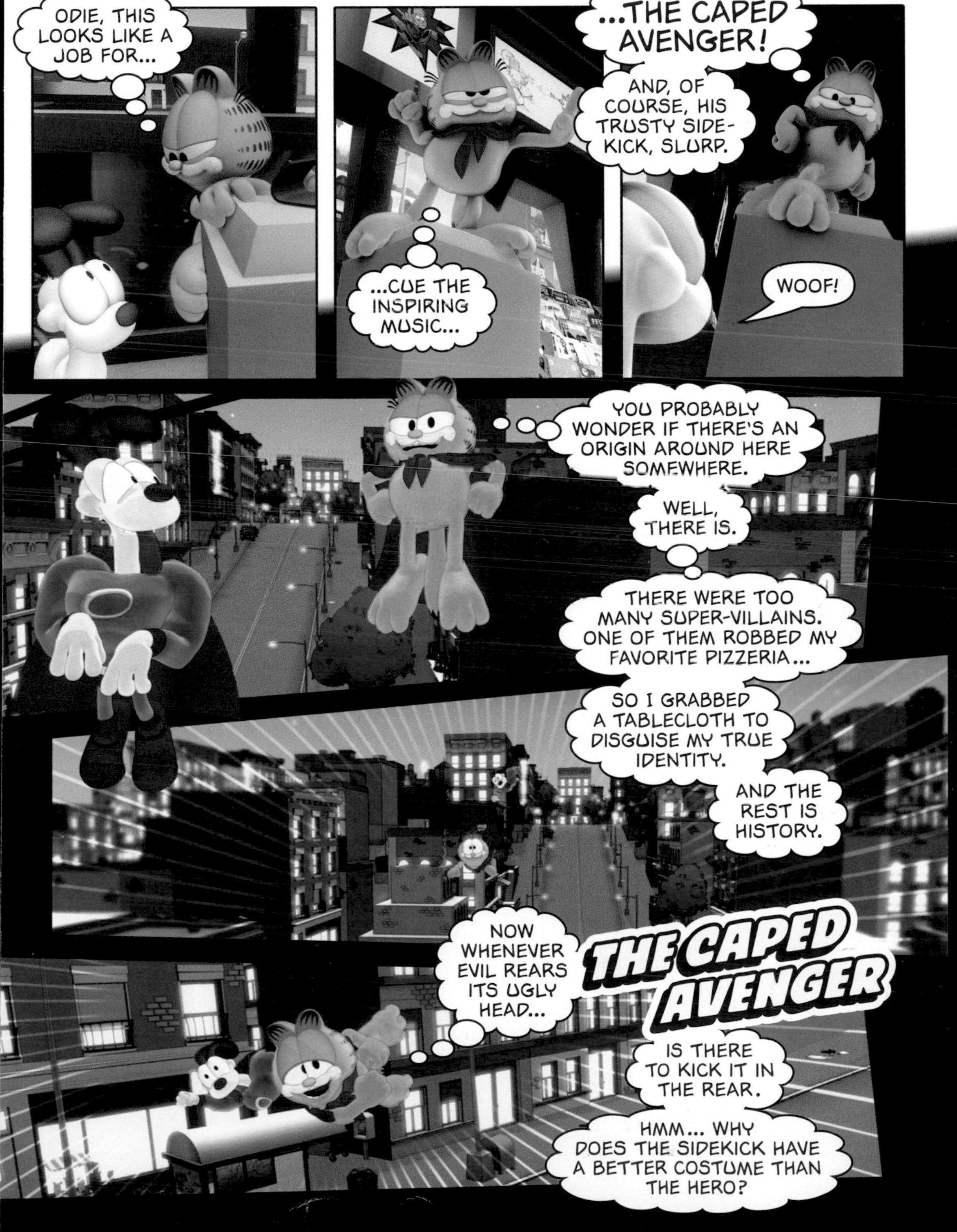
ODIE, THIS LOOKS LIKE A JOB FOR...
...THE CAPED AVENGER!
...CUE THE INSPIRING MUSIC...
AND, OF COURSE, HIS TRUSTY SIDE-KICK, SLURP.
WOOF!
YOU PROBABLY WONDER IF THERE'S AN ORIGIN AROUND HERE SOMEWHERE.
WELL, THERE IS.
THERE WERE TOO MANY SUPER-VILLAINS. ONE OF THEM ROBBED MY FAVORITE PIZZERIA...
SO I GRABBED A TABLECLOTH TO DISGUISE MY TRUE IDENTITY.
AND THE REST IS HISTORY.
NOW WHENEVER EVIL REARS ITS UGLY HEAD...
THE CAPED AVENGER
IS THERE TO KICK IT IN THE REAR.
HMM... WHY DOES THE SIDEKICK HAVE A BETTER COSTUME THAN THE HERO?

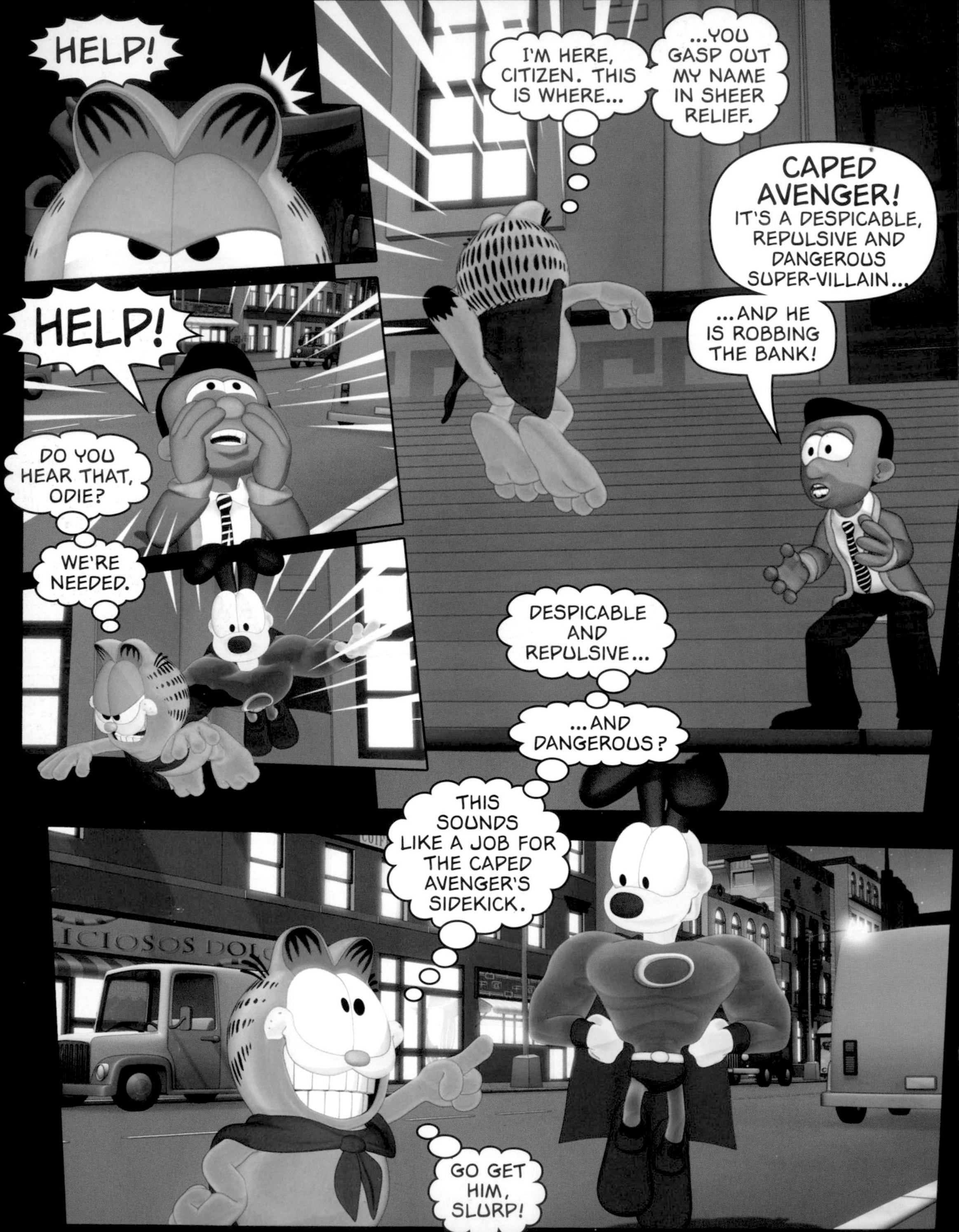
HELP!
HELP!
DO YOU HEAR THAT, ODIE?
WE'RE NEEDED.
I'M HERE, CITIZEN. THIS IS WHERE...
...YOU GASP OUT MY NAME IN SHEER RELIEF.
CAPED AVENGER! IT'S A DESPICABLE, REPULSIVE AND DANGEROUS SUPER-VILLAIN...
...AND HE IS ROBBING THE BANK!
DESPICABLE AND REPULSIVE...
...AND DANGEROUS?
THIS SOUNDS LIKE A JOB FOR THE CAPED AVENGER'S SIDEKICK.
GO GET HIM, SLURP!

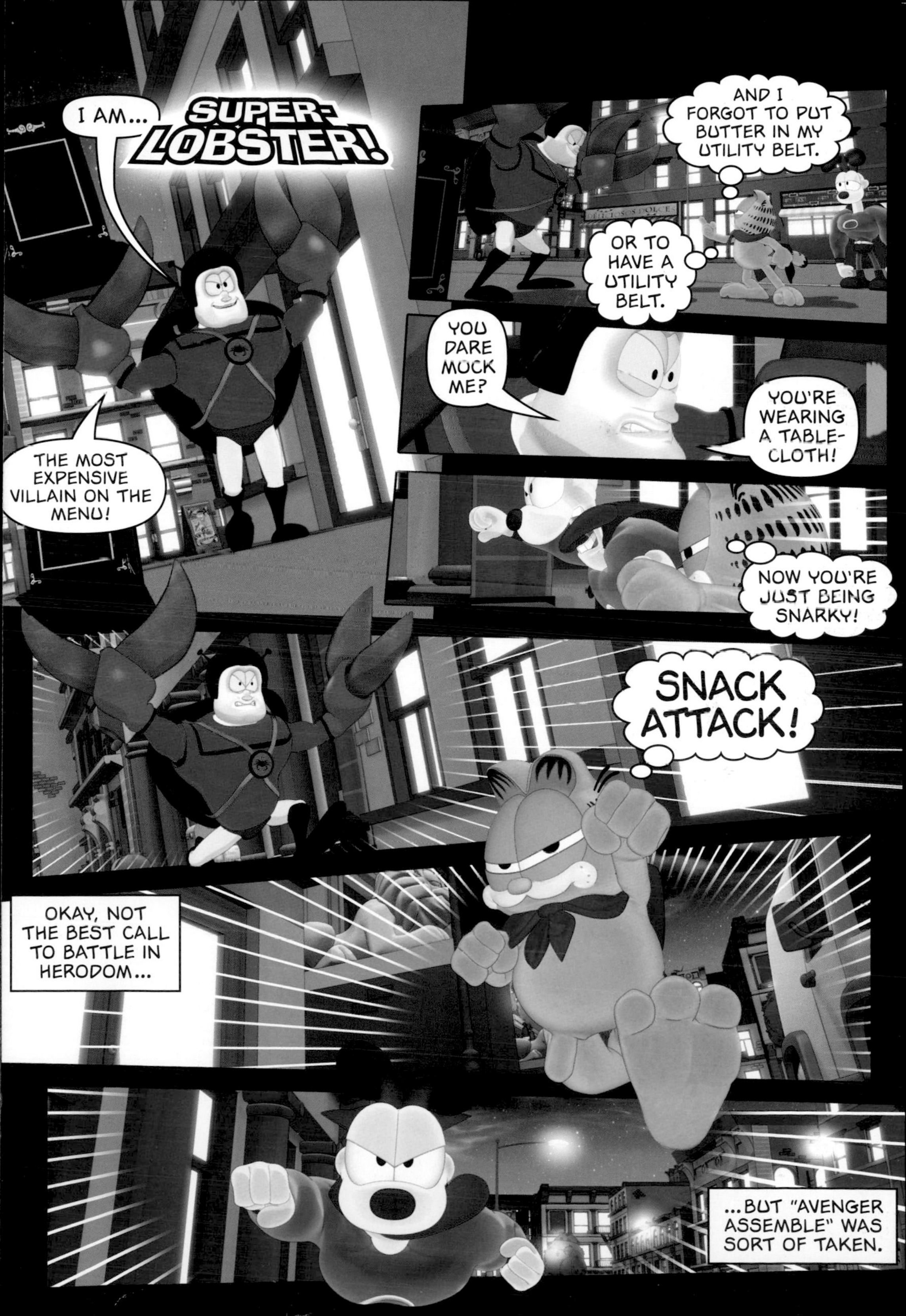

I AM...
SUPER-LOBSTER!
THE MOST EXPENSIVE VILLAIN ON THE MENU!
AND I FORGOT TO PUT BUTTER IN MY UTILITY BELT.
OR TO HAVE A UTILITY BELT.
YOU DARE MOCK ME?
YOU'RE WEARING A TABLE-CLOTH!
NOW YOU'RE JUST BEING SNARKY!
SNACK ATTACK!
OKAY, NOT THE BEST CALL TO BATTLE IN HERODOM...
...BUT "AVENGER ASSEMBLE" WAS SORT OF TAKEN.

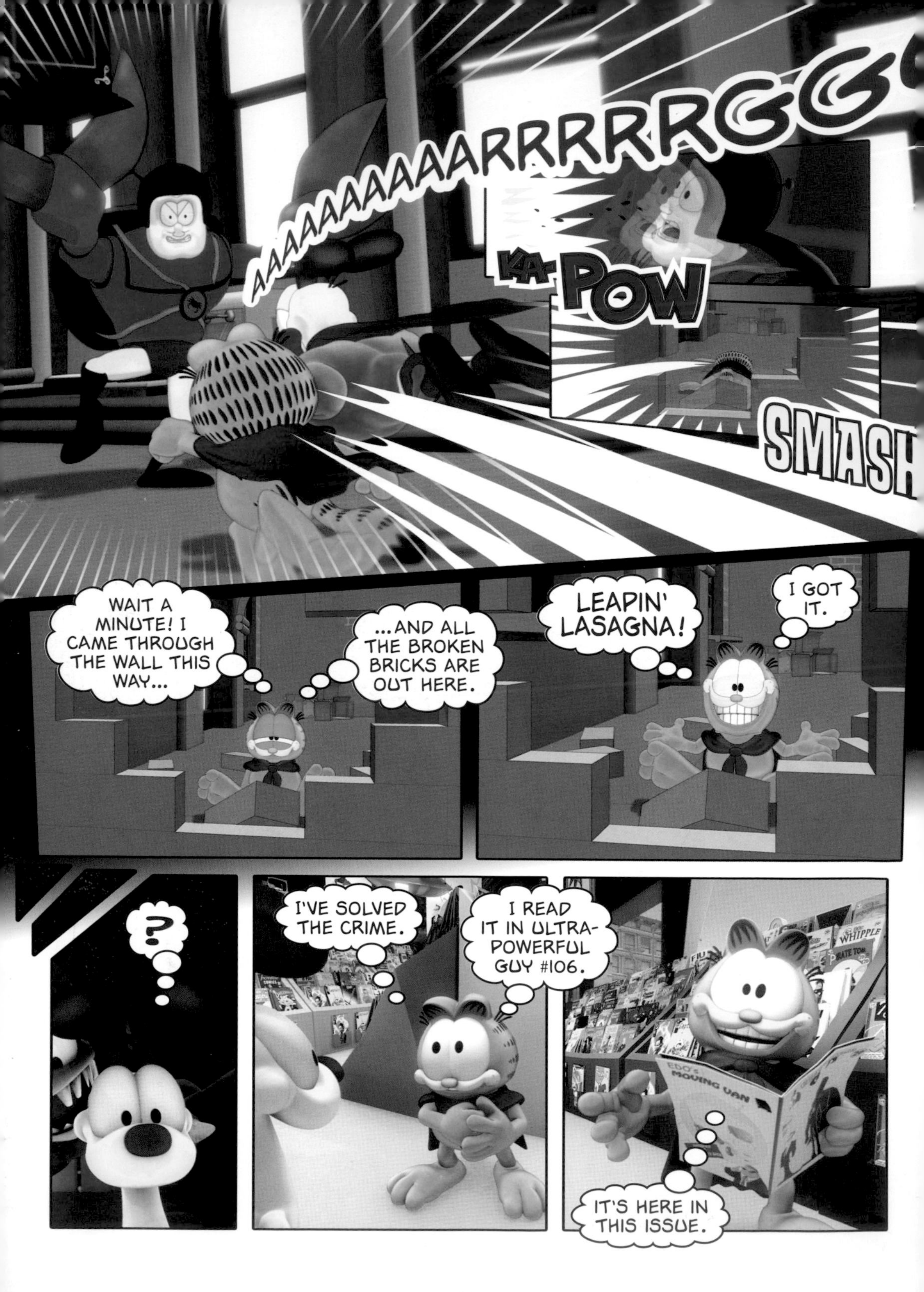
AAAAAAAAAARRRRRRGGG
KA-POW
SMASH
WAIT A MINUTE! I CAME THROUGH THE WALL THIS WAY...
...AND ALL THE BROKEN BRICKS ARE OUT HERE.
LEAPIN' LASAGNA!
I GOT IT.
?
I'VE SOLVED THE CRIME.
I READ IT IN ULTRA-POWERFUL GUY #106.
EDO'S MOVING VAN
IT'S HERE IN THIS ISSUE.

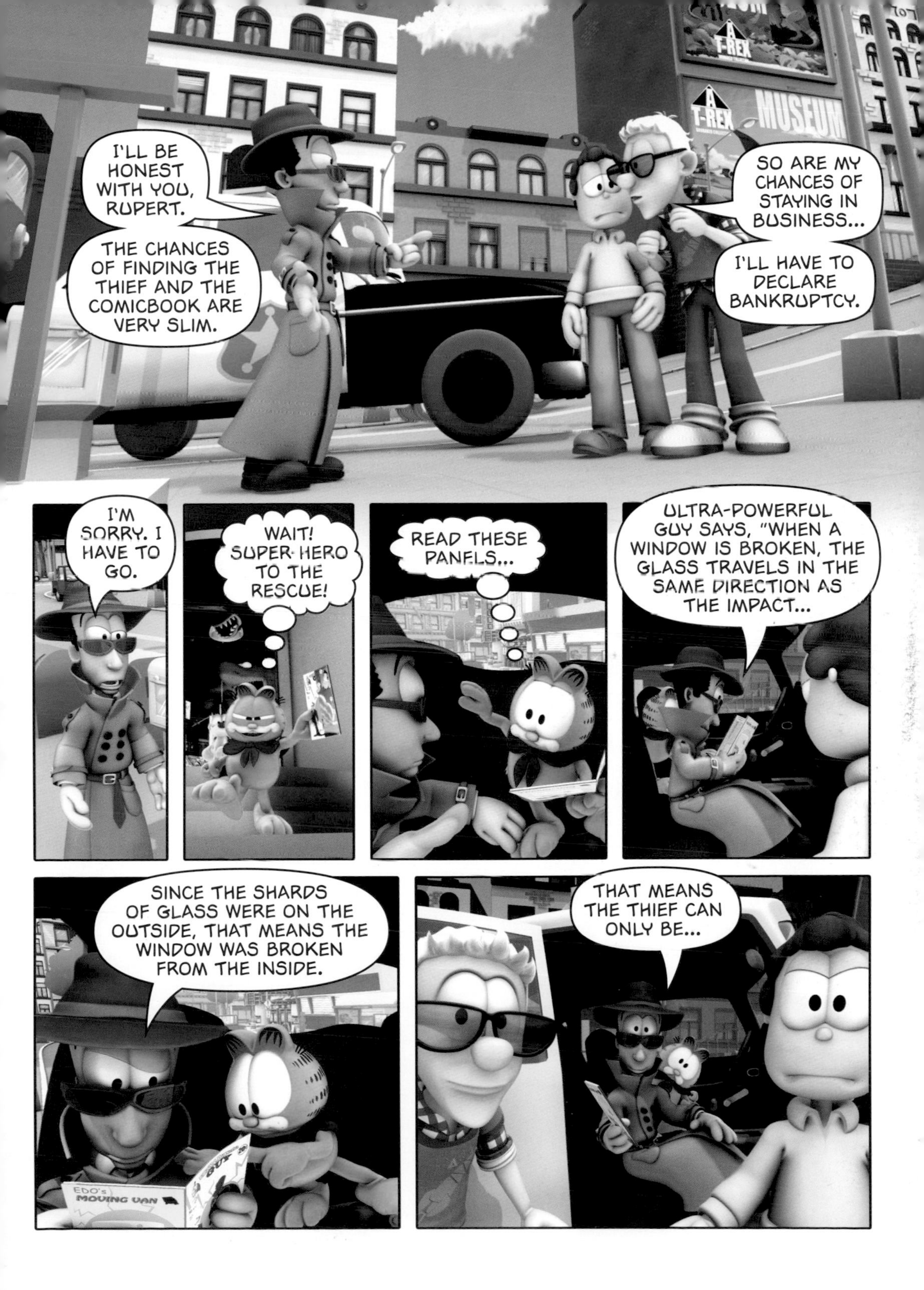
T-REX
MUSEUM
I'LL BE HONEST WITH YOU, RUPERT.
THE CHANCES OF FINDING THE THIEF AND THE COMICBOOK ARE VERY SLIM.
SO ARE MY CHANCES OF STAYING IN BUSINESS...
I'LL HAVE TO DECLARE BANKRUPTCY.
I'M SORRY. I HAVE TO GO.
WAIT! SUPER-HERO TO THE RESCUE!
READ THESE PANELS...
ULTRA-POWERFUL GUY SAYS, "WHEN A WINDOW IS BROKEN, THE GLASS TRAVELS IN THE SAME DIRECTION AS THE IMPACT...
SINCE THE SHARDS OF GLASS WERE ON THE OUTSIDE, THAT MEANS THE WINDOW WAS BROKEN FROM THE INSIDE.
EDO's MOVING VAN
THAT MEANS THE THIEF CAN ONLY BE...

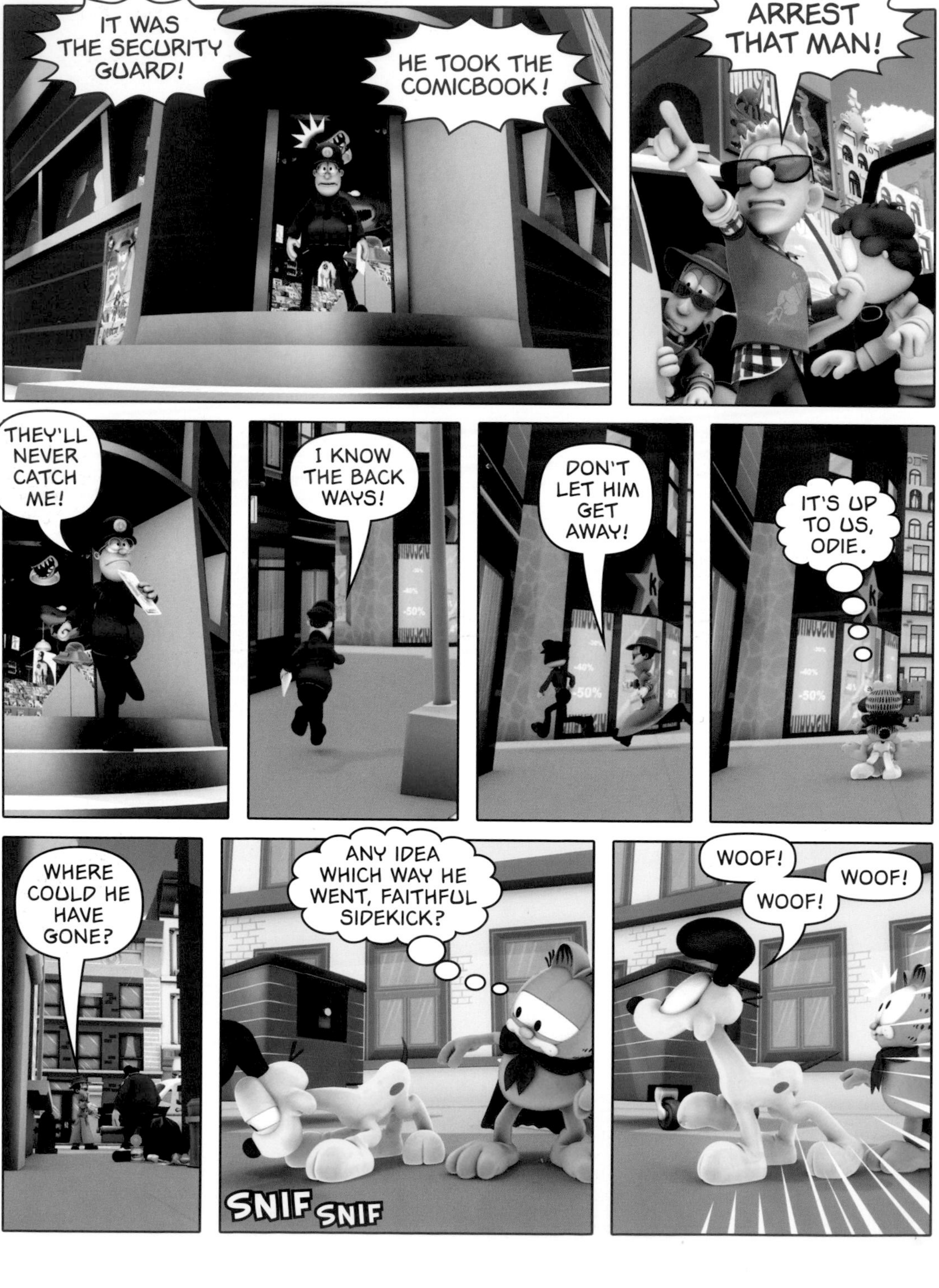
IT WAS THE SECURITY GUARD!
HE TOOK THE COMICBOOK!
ARREST THAT MAN!
THEY'LL NEVER CATCH ME!
I KNOW THE BACK WAYS!
DON'T LET HIM GET AWAY!
IT'S UP TO US, ODIE.
WHERE COULD HE HAVE GONE?
ANY IDEA WHICH WAY HE WENT, FAITHFUL SIDEKICK?
SNIF SNIF
WOOF!
WOOF!
WOOF!

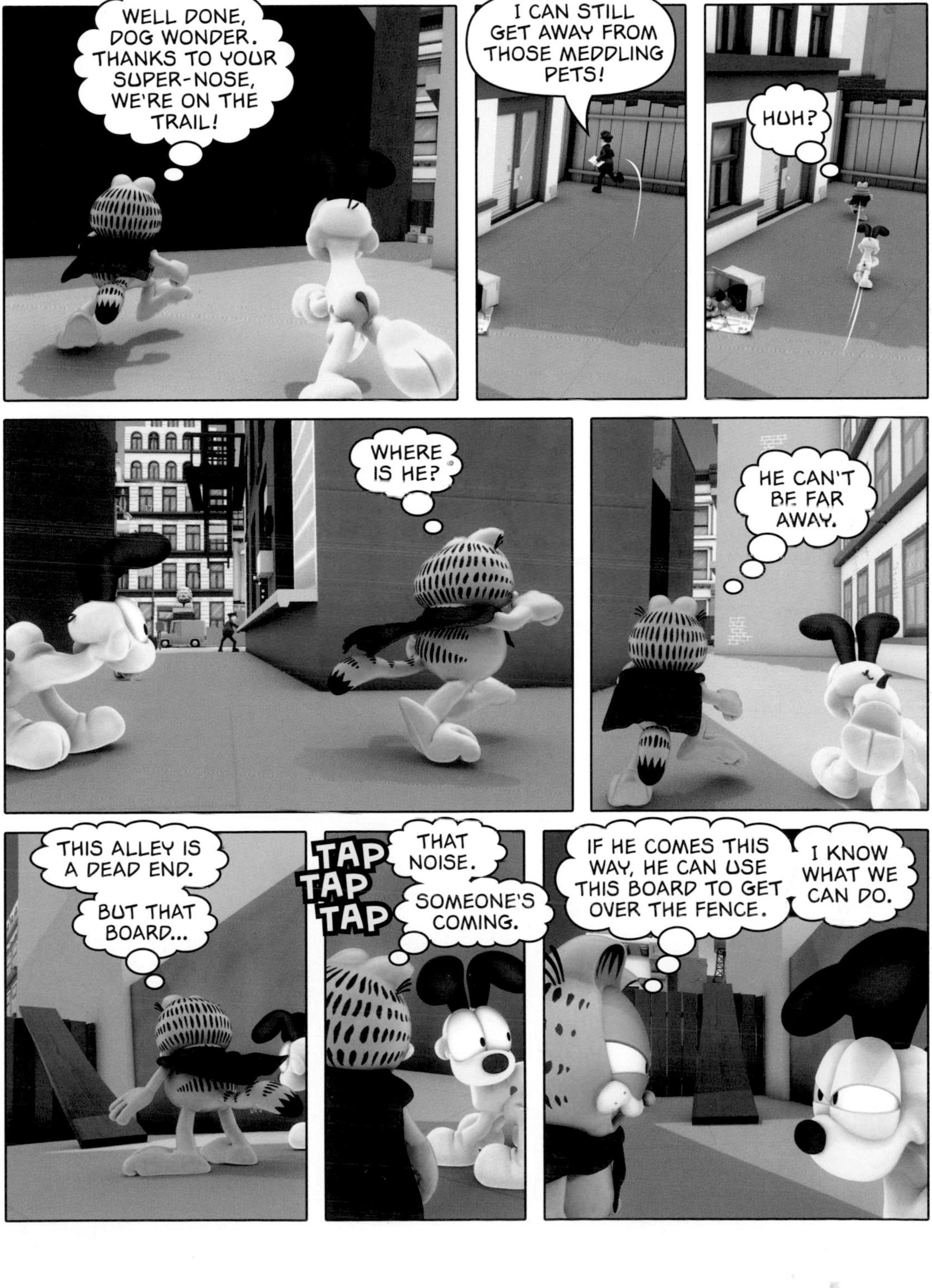
WELL DONE, DOG WONDER. THANKS TO YOUR SUPER-NOSE, WE'RE ON THE TRAIL!
I CAN STILL GET AWAY FROM THOSE MEDDLING PETS!
HUH?
WHERE IS HE?
HE CAN'T BE FAR AWAY.
THIS ALLEY IS A DEAD END.
BUT THAT BOARD...
TAP TAP TAP
THAT NOISE.
SOMEONE'S COMING.
IF HE COMES THIS WAY, HE CAN USE THIS BOARD TO GET OVER THE FENCE.
I KNOW WHAT WE CAN DO.

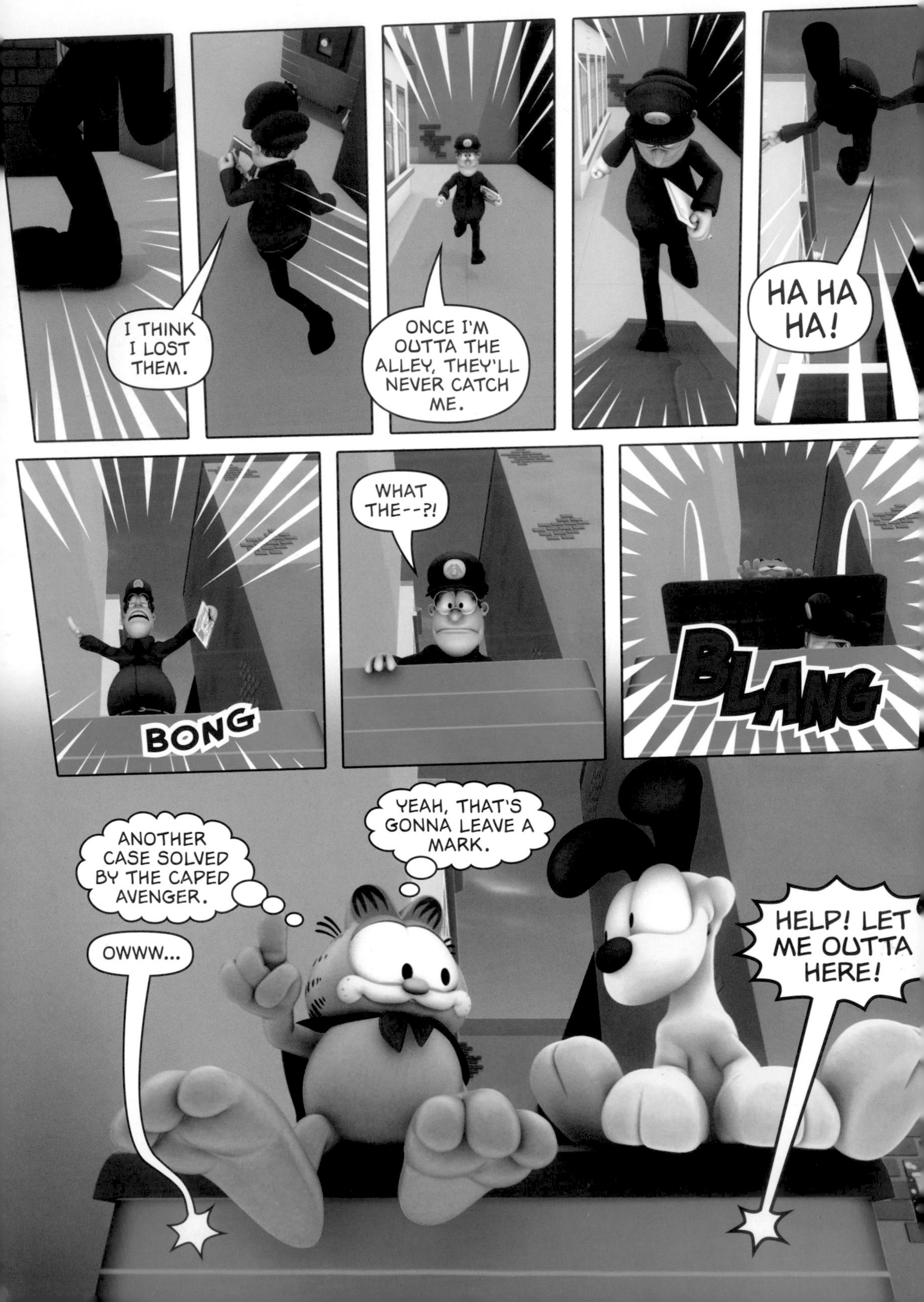
I THINK I LOST THEM.
ONCE I'M OUTTA THE ALLEY, THEY'LL NEVER CATCH ME.
HA HA HA!
BONG
WHAT THE--?!
BLANG
ANOTHER CASE SOLVED BY THE CAPED AVENGER.
YEAH, THAT'S GONNA LEAVE A MARK.
OWWW...
HELP! LET ME OUTTA HERE!

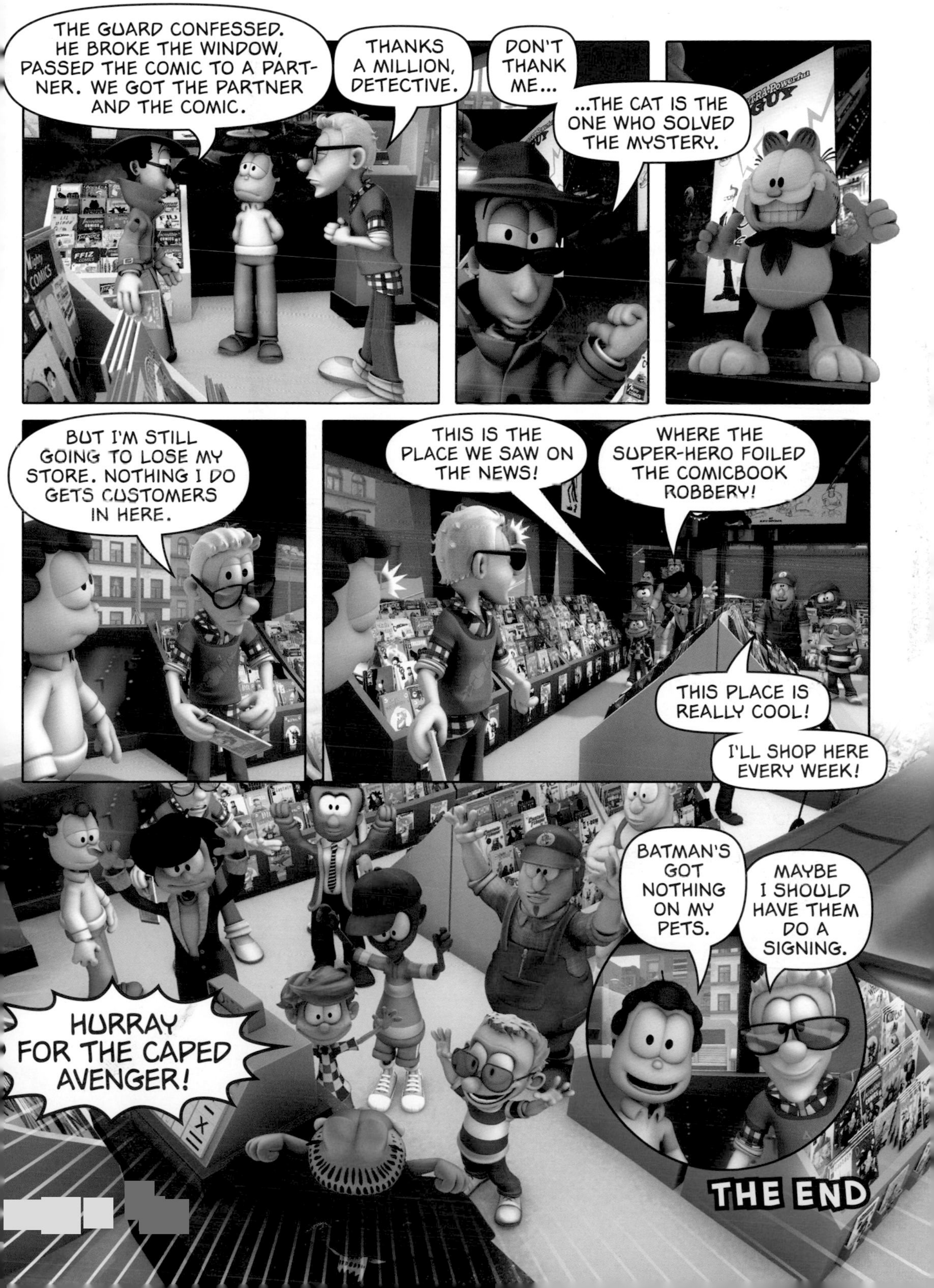
THE GUARD CONFESSED. HE BROKE THE WINDOW, PASSED THE COMIC TO A PART- NER. WE GOT THE PARTNER AND THE COMIC.
THANKS A MILLION, DETECTIVE.
DON'T THANK ME...
...THE CAT IS THE ONE WHO SOLVED THE MYSTERY.
BUT I'M STILL GOING TO LOSE MY STORE. NOTHING I DO GETS CUSTOMERS IN HERE.
THIS IS THE PLACE WE SAW ON THE NEWS!
WHERE THE SUPER-HERO FOILED THE COMICBOOK ROBBERY!
THIS PLACE IS REALLY COOL!
I'LL SHOP HERE EVERY WEEK!
HURRAY FOR THE CAPED AVENGER!
BATMAN'S GOT NOTHING ON MY PETS.
MAYBE I SHOULD HAVE THEM DO A SIGNING.
THE END

# WATCH OUT FOR PAPERCUTZ

CARICATURE OF JIM
BY ORTHO

Welcome to the fabulously fit fifth THE GARFIELD SHOW graphic novel from Papercutz, the kind-hearted cat lovers devoted to publishing great graphic novels for all ages. I'm Jim Salicrup, Editor-in-Chief and President of the Ultra-Powerful Guy Appreciation Society, New York City Chapter, here to talk once again about a few other cartoon cats, cats we like to call THE PAPERCATZ…

If you recall, we talked about a few other cartoon cats also published by Papercutz in THE GARFIELD SHOW #4 "Little Trouble in Big China." Cats such as Azrael (that wicked wizard Gargamel's long-suffering cat from THE SMURFS), the Pirate Cats (those time-travelling baddies from GERONIMO STILTON), and another, perhaps lesser known feline known simply as Pussycat. We thought it might be fun to present a sample of the Pussycat comic strip right here…

If you recognize the name Peyo, that's the *nom de plume* of cartoonist Pierre Culliford, the creator of THE SMURFS. PUSSYCAT is one of his earlier works, and Papercutz is proud to be collecting all of the PUSSYCAT strips in one big deluxe hardcover book, similar to our much-praised THE SMURFS ANTHOLOGY books.

PHOTO © 2010 BY LOIS BUHALIS

One final note, for all the fans of comics lettering, we're happy to welcome back award-winning letterer Tom Orzechowski. Tom went above and beyond the call of duty working on this volume, and we want to sincerely thank him. We'll all be back in THE GARFIELD SHOW #6 "Stink, Stank, Stunk!" and hope you'll be here too!

Thanks,

Jim

© Peyo - 2015 - Licensed through Lafig Belgium - www.smurf.com

**STAY IN TOUCH!**

EMAIL: SALICRUP@PAPERCUTZ.COM
WEB: PAPERCUTZ.COM
TWITTER: @PAPERCUTZGN
FACEBOOK: PAPERCUTZGRAPHICNOVELS
BIRTHDAY CARDS: PAPERCUTZ, 160 BROADWAY, SUITE 700, EAST WING, NEW YORK, NY 10038

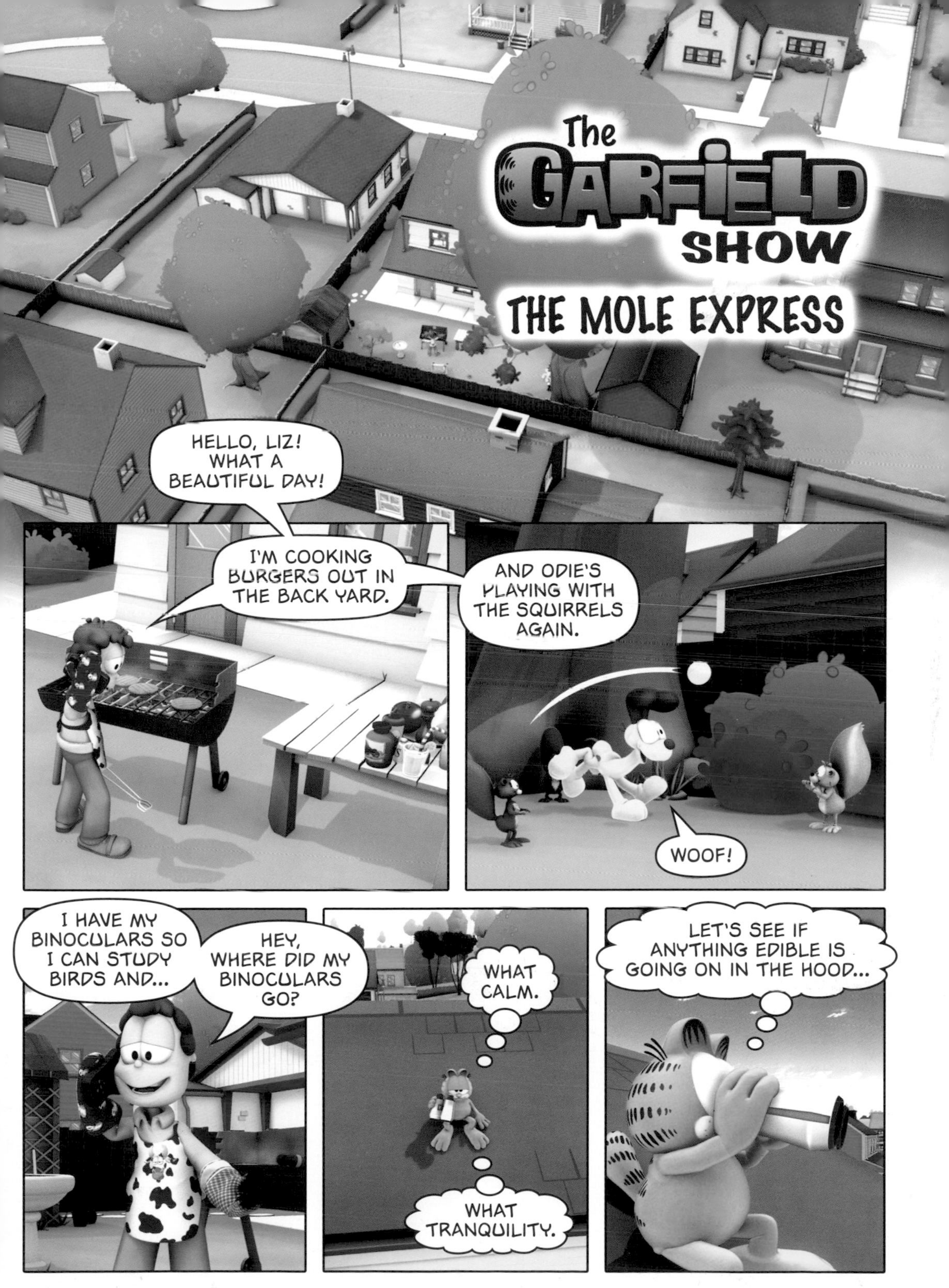
The
GARFIELD
SHOW
THE MOLE EXPRESS
HELLO, LIZ! WHAT A BEAUTIFUL DAY!
I'M COOKING BURGERS OUT IN THE BACK YARD.
AND ODIE'S PLAYING WITH THE SQUIRRELS AGAIN.
WOOF!
I HAVE MY BINOCULARS SO I CAN STUDY BIRDS AND...
HEY, WHERE DID MY BINOCULARS GO?
WHAT CALM.
WHAT TRANQUILITY.
LET'S SEE IF ANYTHING EDIBLE IS GOING ON IN THE HOOD...

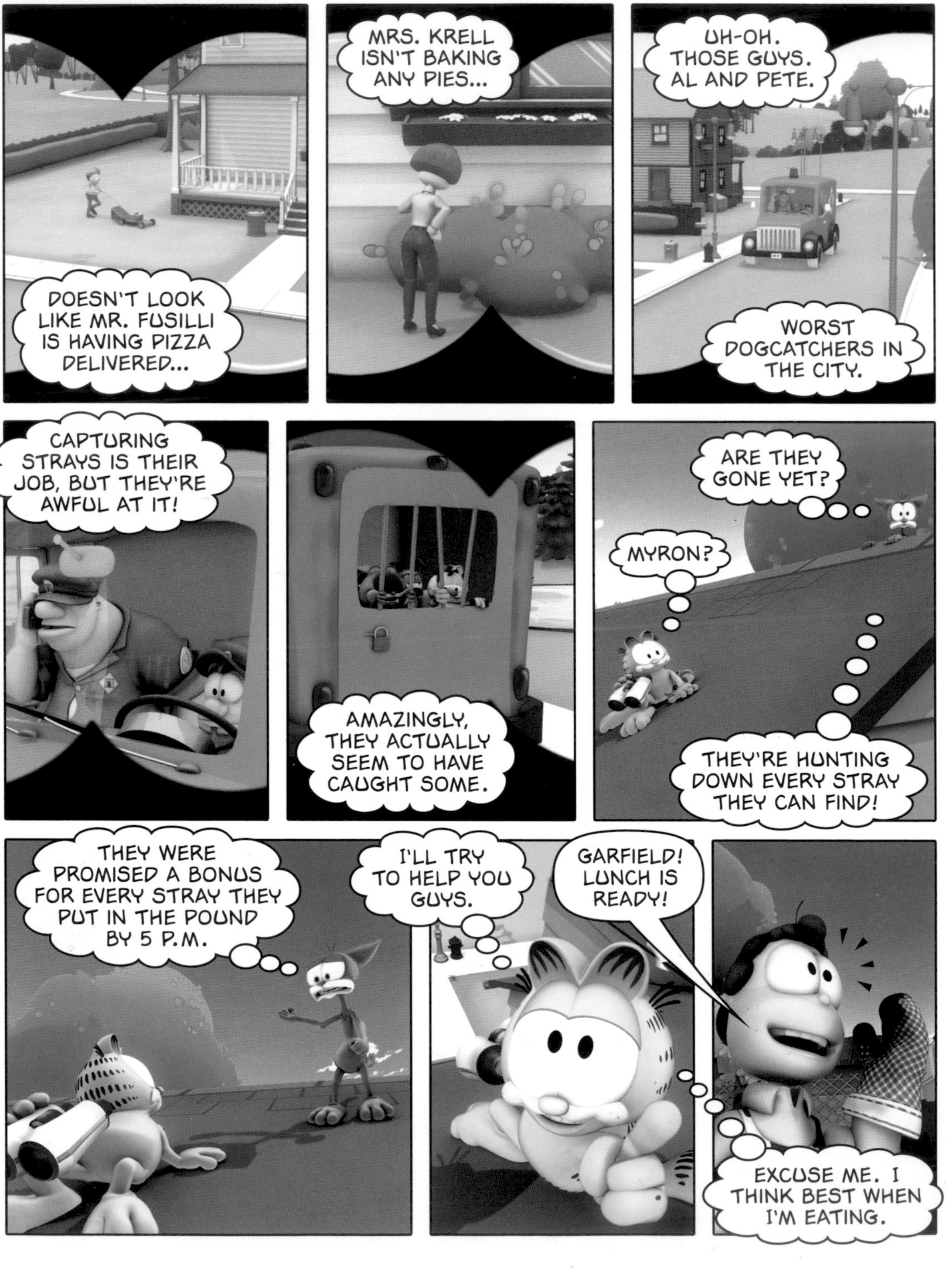
DOESN'T LOOK LIKE MR. FUSILLI IS HAVING PIZZA DELIVERED...
MRS. KRELL ISN'T BAKING ANY PIES...
UH-OH. THOSE GUYS. AL AND PETE.
WORST DOGCATCHERS IN THE CITY.
CAPTURING STRAYS IS THEIR JOB, BUT THEY'RE AWFUL AT IT!
AMAZINGLY, THEY ACTUALLY SEEM TO HAVE CAUGHT SOME.
ARE THEY GONE YET?
MYRON?
THEY'RE HUNTING DOWN EVERY STRAY THEY CAN FIND!
THEY WERE PROMISED A BONUS FOR EVERY STRAY THEY PUT IN THE POUND BY 5 P.M.
I'LL TRY TO HELP YOU GUYS.
GARFIELD! LUNCH IS READY!
EXCUSE ME. I THINK BEST WHEN I'M EATING.

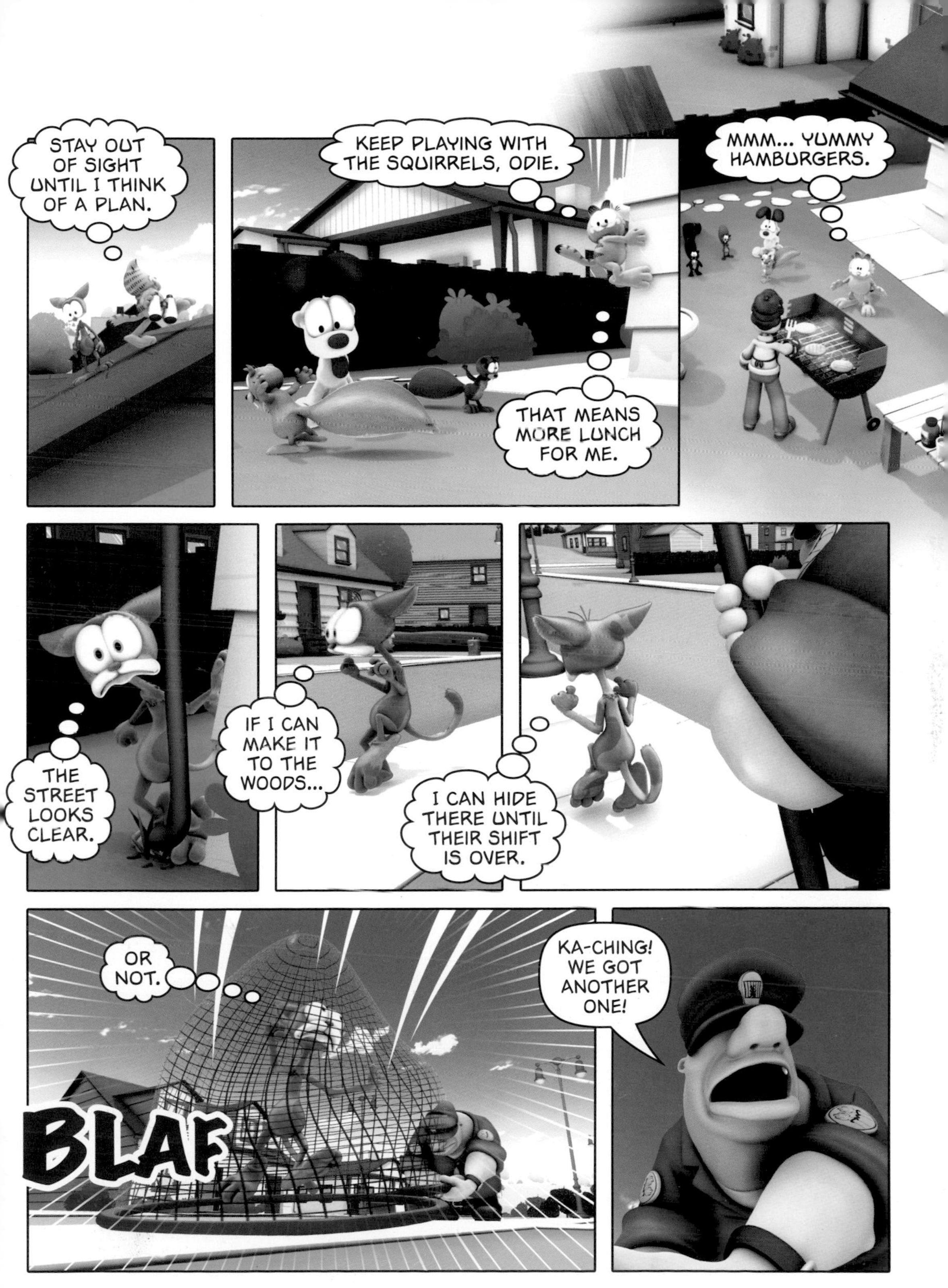
STAY OUT OF SIGHT UNTIL I THINK OF A PLAN.
KEEP PLAYING WITH THE SQUIRRELS, ODIE.
THAT MEANS MORE LUNCH FOR ME.
MMM... YUMMY HAMBURGERS.
THE STREET LOOKS CLEAR.
IF I CAN MAKE IT TO THE WOODS...
I CAN HIDE THERE UNTIL THEIR SHIFT IS OVER.
OR NOT.
BLAF
KA-CHING! WE GOT ANOTHER ONE!

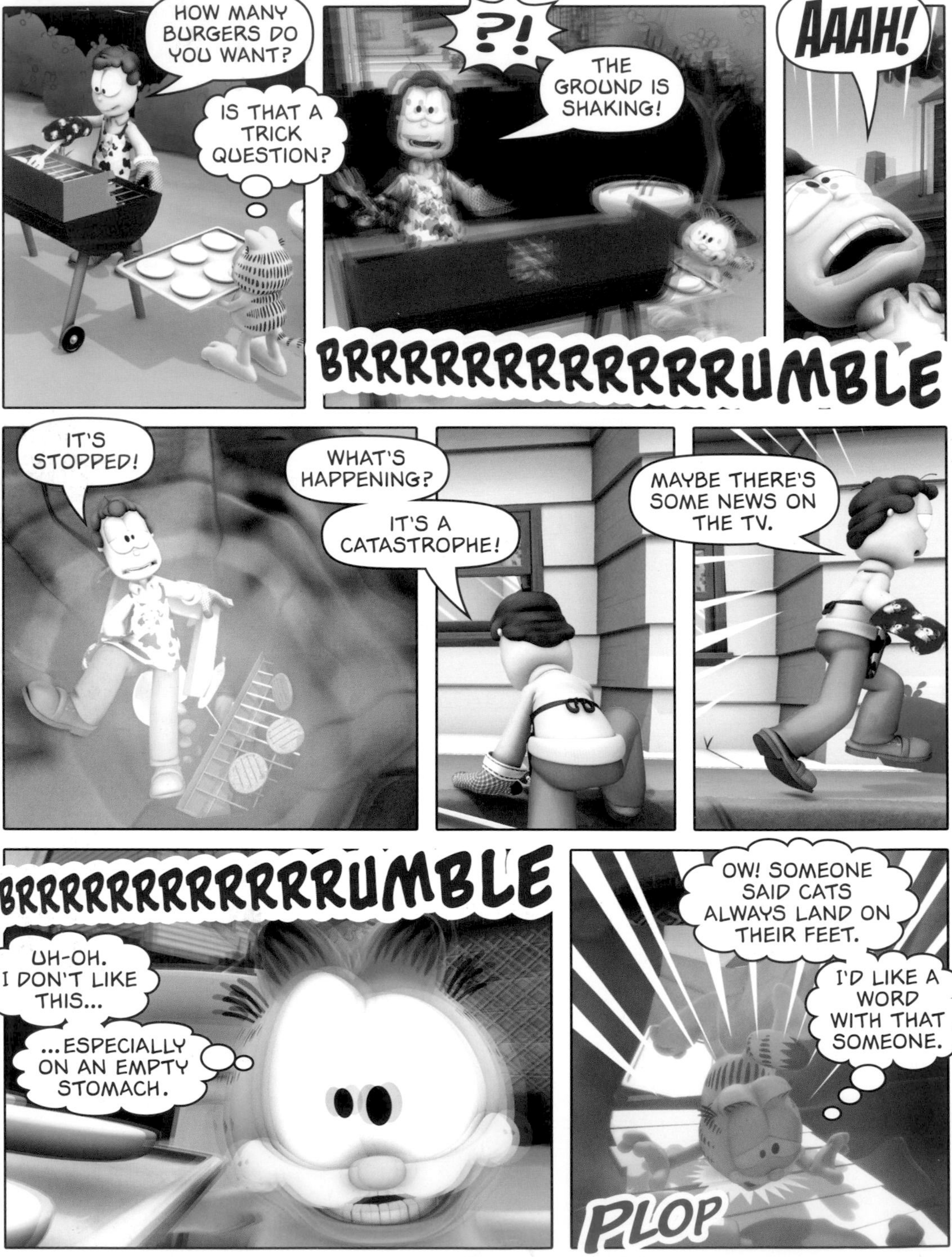
HOW MANY BURGERS DO YOU WANT?
IS THAT A TRICK QUESTION?
?!
THE GROUND IS SHAKING!
AAAH!
BRRRRRRRRRRRRRUMBLE
IT'S STOPPED!
WHAT'S HAPPENING?
IT'S A CATASTROPHE!
MAYBE THERE'S SOME NEWS ON THE TV.
BRRRRRRRRRRRRRUMBLE
UH-OH. I DON'T LIKE THIS...
...ESPECIALLY ON AN EMPTY STOMACH.
OW! SOMEONE SAID CATS ALWAYS LAND ON THEIR FEET.
I'D LIKE A WORD WITH THAT SOMEONE.
PLOP

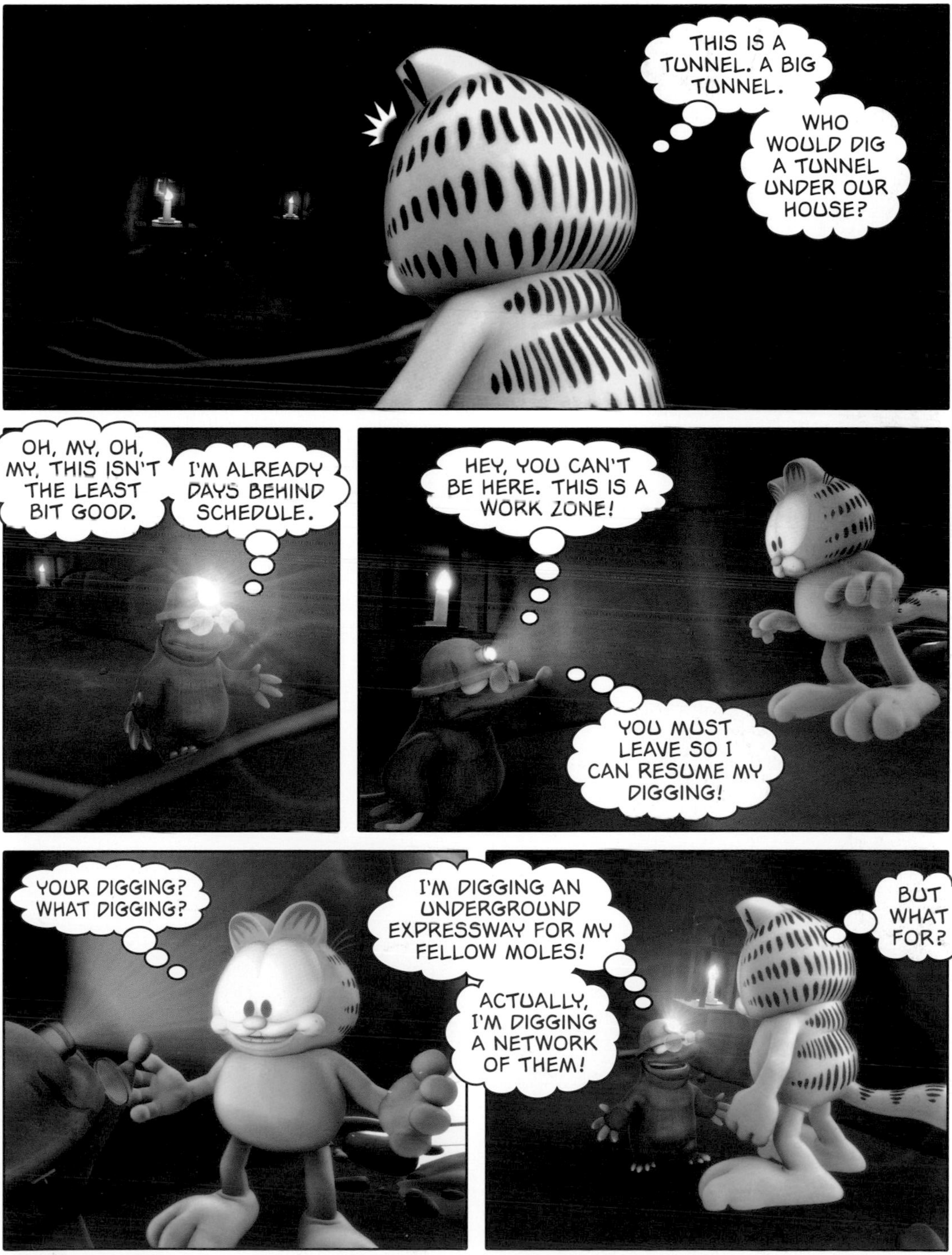
THIS IS A TUNNEL. A BIG TUNNEL.
WHO WOULD DIG A TUNNEL UNDER OUR HOUSE?
OH, MY, OH, MY, THIS ISN'T THE LEAST BIT GOOD.
I'M ALREADY DAYS BEHIND SCHEDULE.
HEY, YOU CAN'T BE HERE. THIS IS A WORK ZONE!
YOU MUST LEAVE SO I CAN RESUME MY DIGGING!
YOUR DIGGING? WHAT DIGGING?
I'M DIGGING AN UNDERGROUND EXPRESSWAY FOR MY FELLOW MOLES!
ACTUALLY, I'M DIGGING A NETWORK OF THEM!
BUT WHAT FOR?

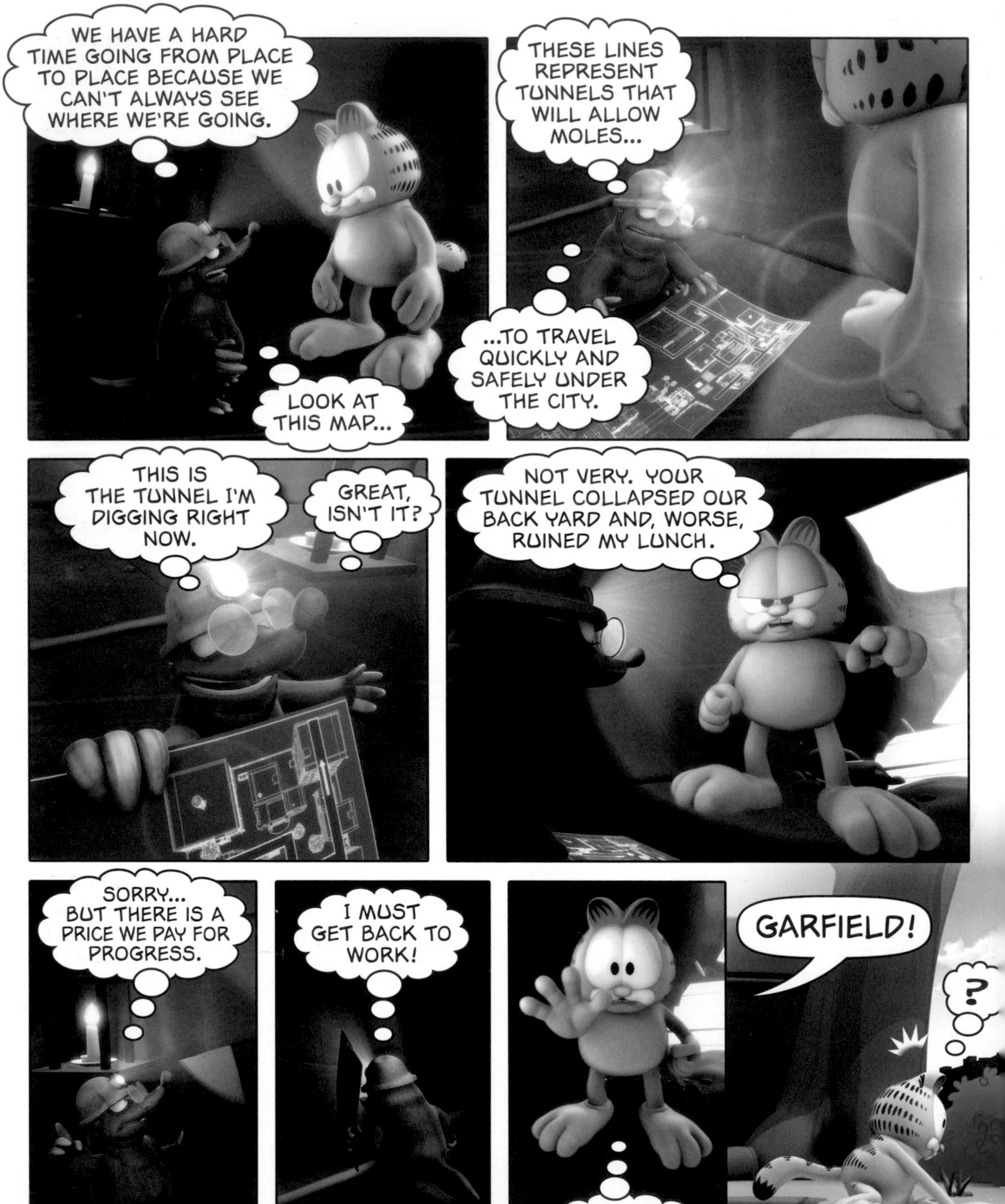
WE HAVE A HARD TIME GOING FROM PLACE TO PLACE BECAUSE WE CAN'T ALWAYS SEE WHERE WE'RE GOING.
LOOK AT THIS MAP...
THESE LINES REPRESENT TUNNELS THAT WILL ALLOW MOLES...
...TO TRAVEL QUICKLY AND SAFELY UNDER THE CITY.
THIS IS THE TUNNEL I'M DIGGING RIGHT NOW.
GREAT, ISN'T IT?
NOT VERY. YOUR TUNNEL COLLAPSED OUR BACK YARD AND, WORSE, RUINED MY LUNCH.
SORRY... BUT THERE IS A PRICE WE PAY FOR PROGRESS.
I MUST GET BACK TO WORK!
WAIT! WE NEED TO TALK!
GARFIELD!
?

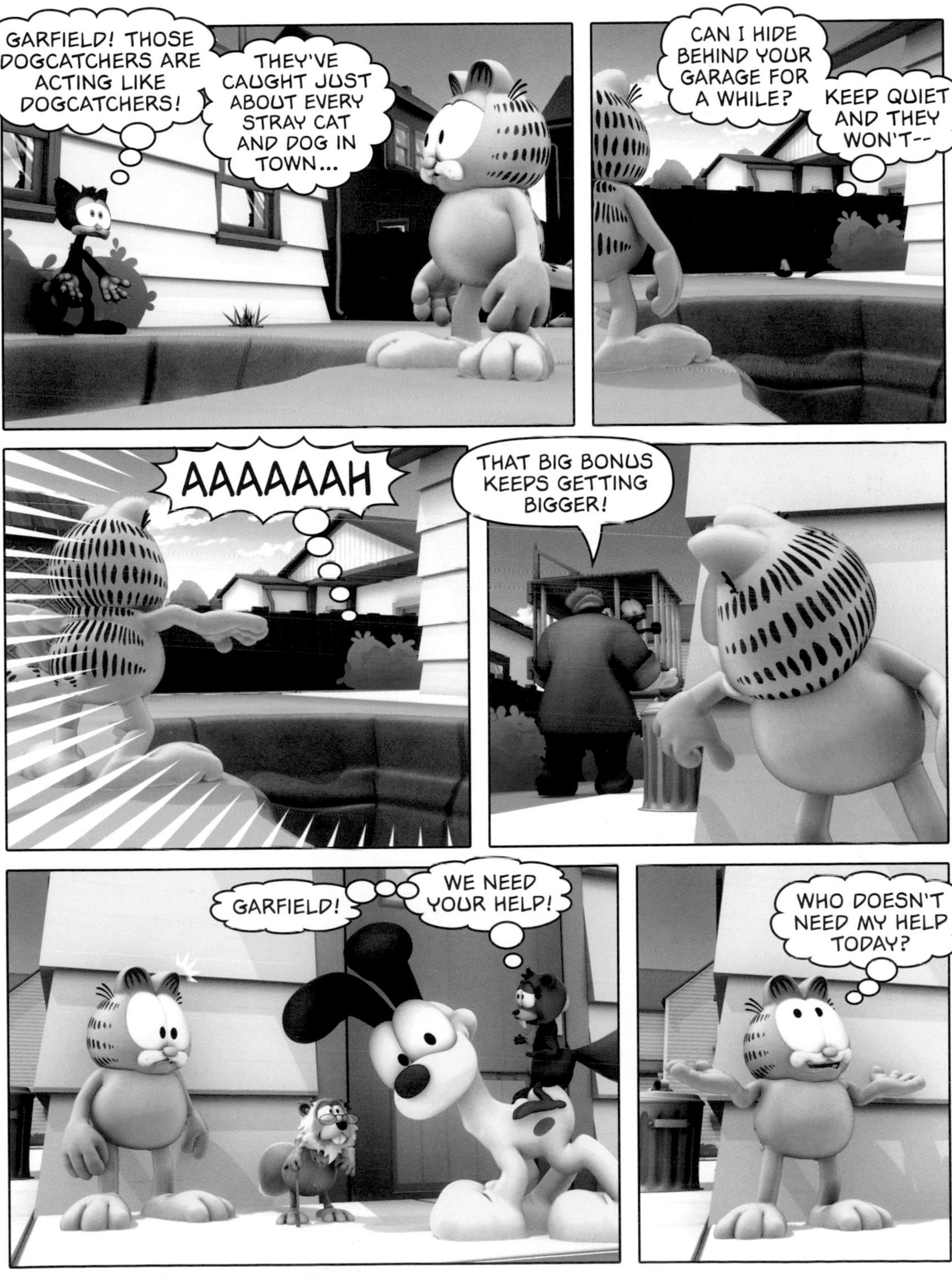
GARFIELD! THOSE DOGCATCHERS ARE ACTING LIKE DOGCATCHERS!
THEY'VE CAUGHT JUST ABOUT EVERY STRAY CAT AND DOG IN TOWN...
CAN I HIDE BEHIND YOUR GARAGE FOR A WHILE?
KEEP QUIET AND THEY WON'T--
AAAAAAH
THAT BIG BONUS KEEPS GETTING BIGGER!
GARFIELD!
WE NEED YOUR HELP!
WHO DOESN'T NEED MY HELP TODAY?

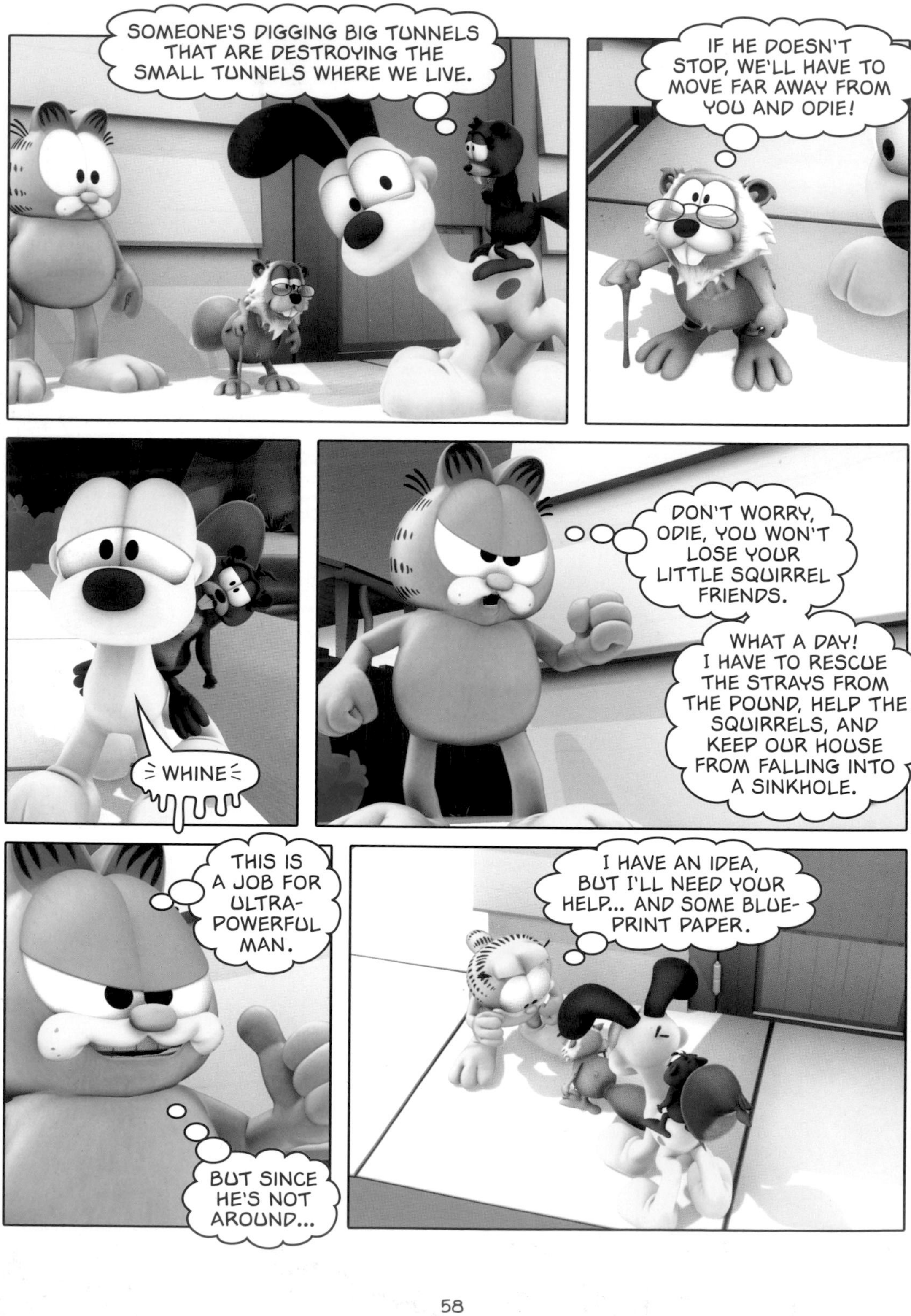
SOMEONE'S DIGGING BIG TUNNELS THAT ARE DESTROYING THE SMALL TUNNELS WHERE WE LIVE.
IF HE DOESN'T STOP, WE'LL HAVE TO MOVE FAR AWAY FROM YOU AND ODIE!
WHINE
DON'T WORRY, ODIE, YOU WON'T LOSE YOUR LITTLE SQUIRREL FRIENDS.
WHAT A DAY! I HAVE TO RESCUE THE STRAYS FROM THE POUND, HELP THE SQUIRRELS, AND KEEP OUR HOUSE FROM FALLING INTO A SINKHOLE.
THIS IS A JOB FOR ULTRA-POWERFUL MAN.
BUT SINCE HE'S NOT AROUND...
I HAVE AN IDEA, BUT I'LL NEED YOUR HELP... AND SOME BLUE-PRINT PAPER.

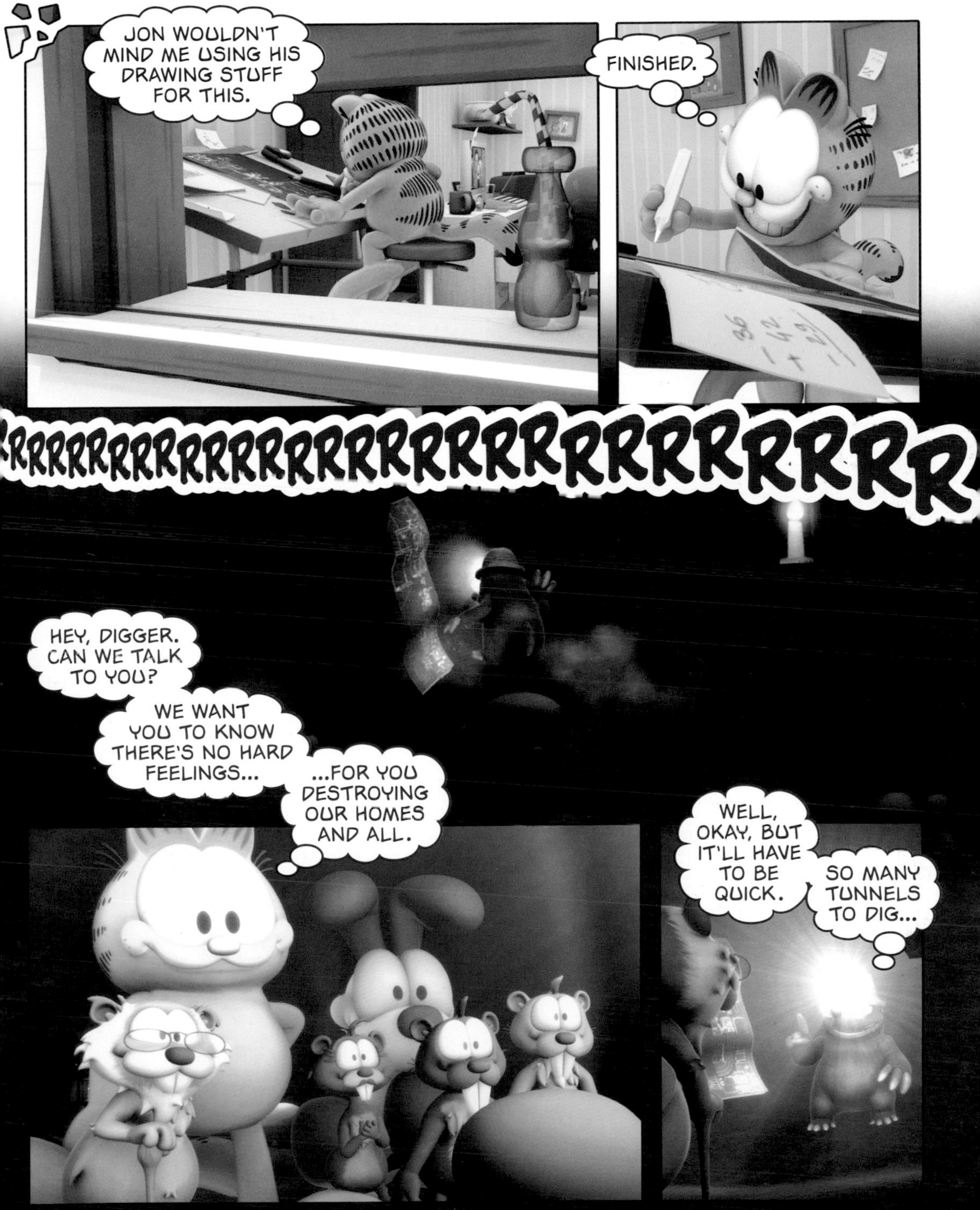
JON WOULDN'T MIND ME USING HIS DRAWING STUFF FOR THIS.
FINISHED.
RRRRRRRRRRRRRRRRRRRRRRRRRRRR
HEY, DIGGER. CAN WE TALK TO YOU?
WE WANT YOU TO KNOW THERE'S NO HARD FEELINGS...
...FOR YOU DESTROYING OUR HOMES AND ALL.
WELL, OKAY, BUT IT'LL HAVE TO BE QUICK.
SO MANY TUNNELS TO DIG...

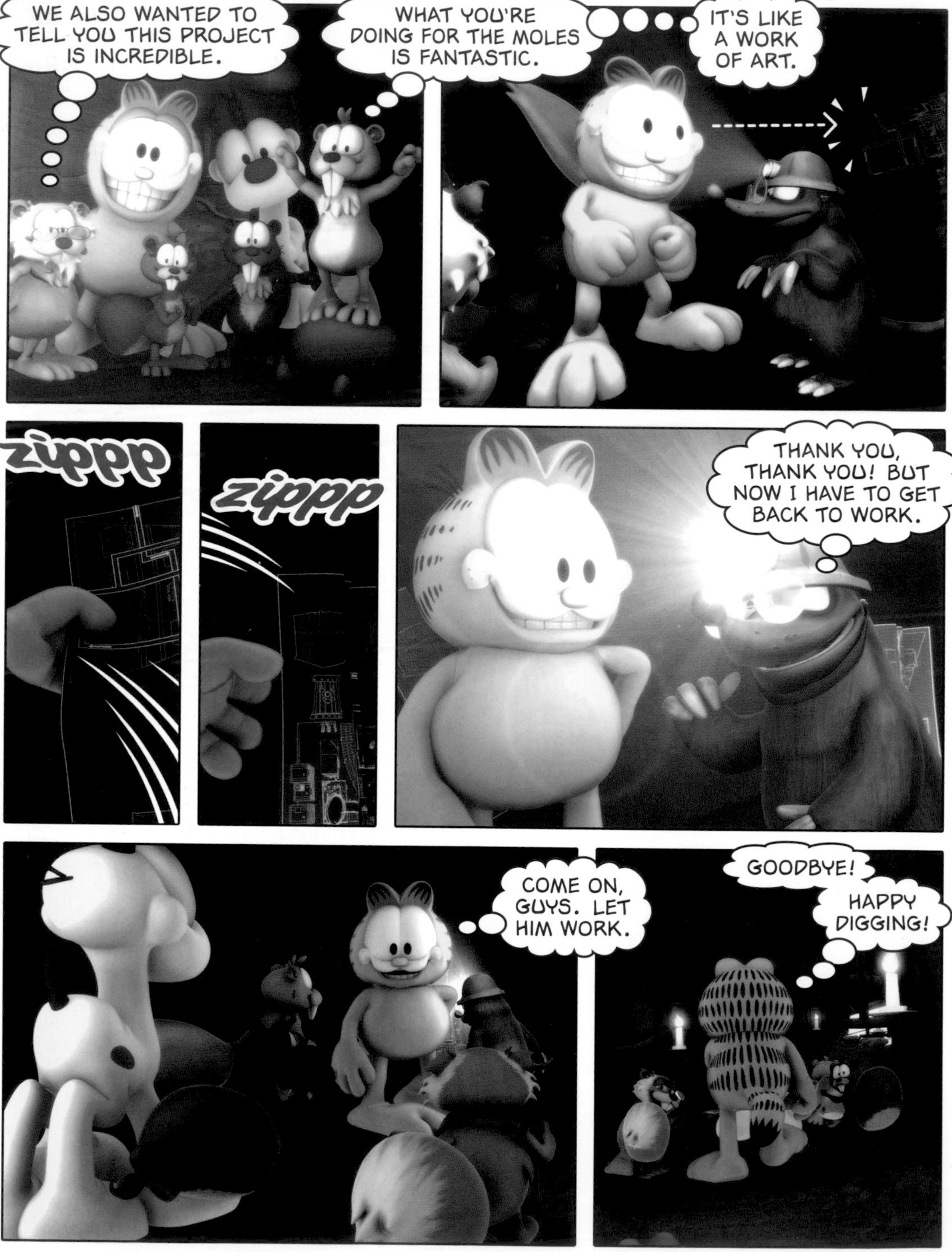
WE ALSO WANTED TO TELL YOU THIS PROJECT IS INCREDIBLE.
WHAT YOU'RE DOING FOR THE MOLES IS FANTASTIC.
IT'S LIKE A WORK OF ART.
ZIPPP
ZIPPP
THANK YOU, THANK YOU! BUT NOW I HAVE TO GET BACK TO WORK.
COME ON, GUYS. LET HIM WORK.
GOODBYE!
HAPPY DIGGING!

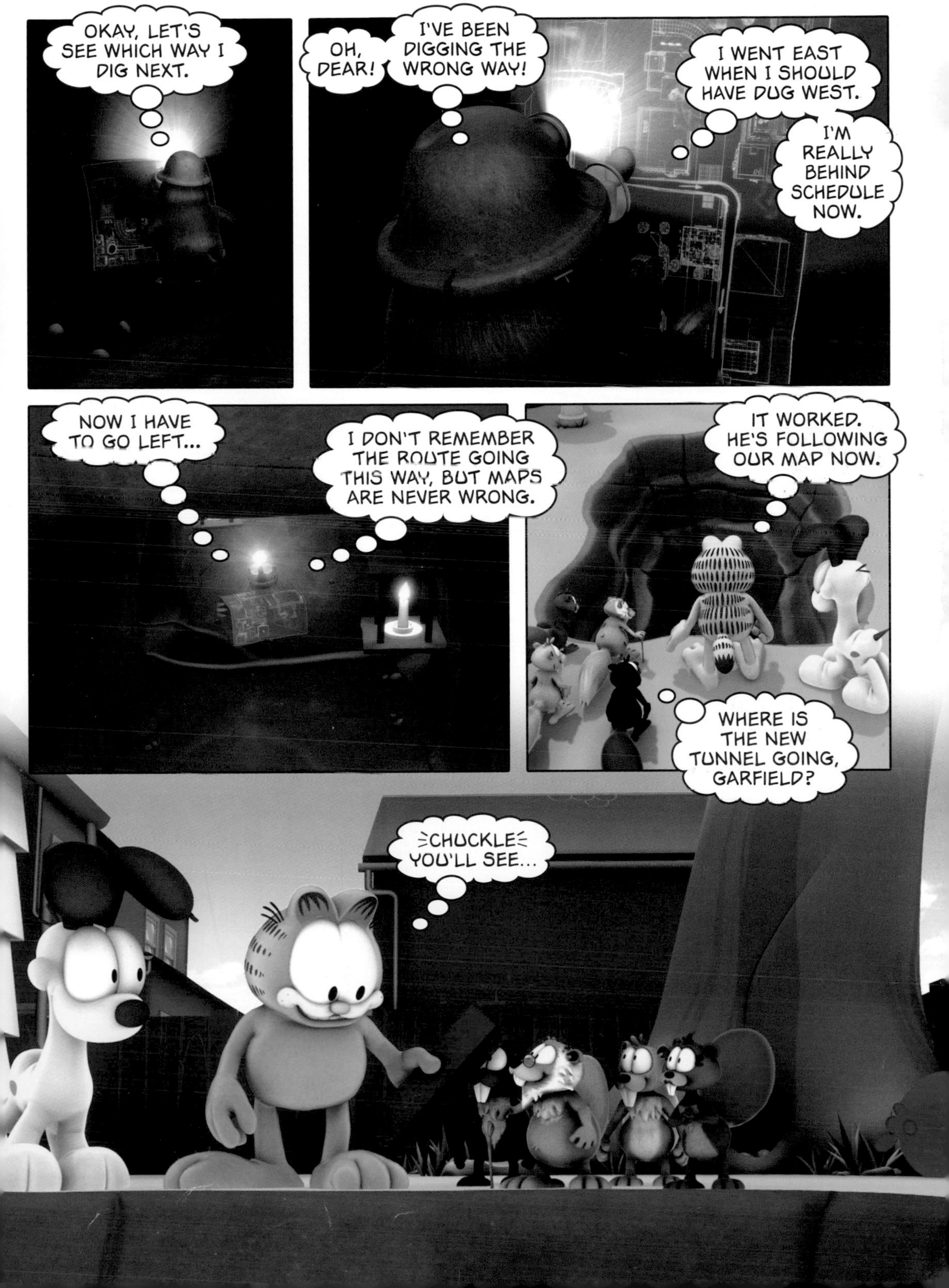
OKAY, LET'S SEE WHICH WAY I DIG NEXT.
OH, DEAR!
I'VE BEEN DIGGING THE WRONG WAY!
I WENT EAST WHEN I SHOULD HAVE DUG WEST.
I'M REALLY BEHIND SCHEDULE NOW.
NOW I HAVE TO GO LEFT...
I DON'T REMEMBER THE ROUTE GOING THIS WAY, BUT MAPS ARE NEVER WRONG.
IT WORKED. HE'S FOLLOWING OUR MAP NOW.
WHERE IS THE NEW TUNNEL GOING, GARFIELD?
CHUCKLE
YOU'LL SEE...

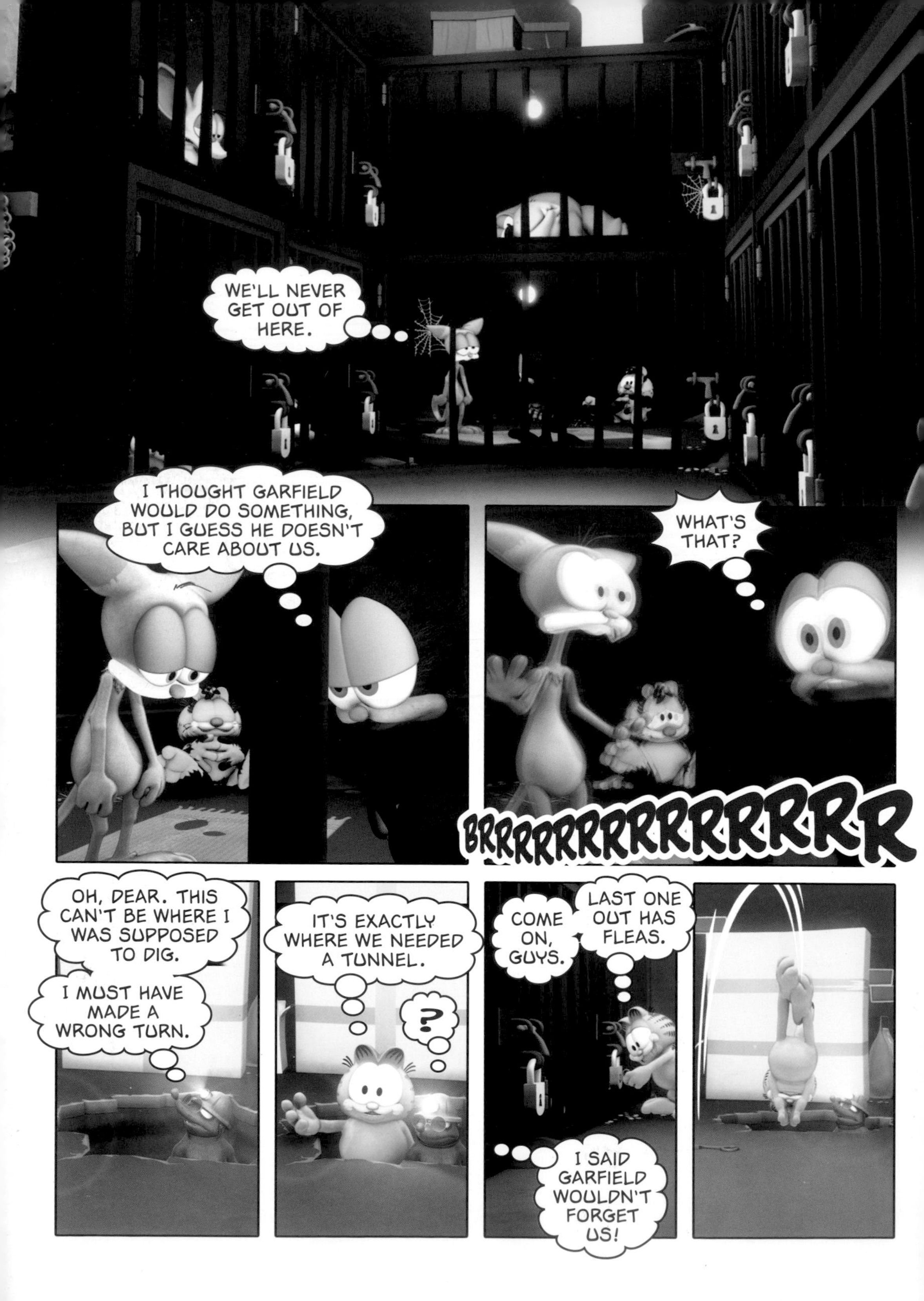

WE'LL NEVER GET OUT OF HERE.
I THOUGHT GARFIELD WOULD DO SOMETHING, BUT I GUESS HE DOESN'T CARE ABOUT US.
WHAT'S THAT?
BRRRRRRRRRRRRRR
OH, DEAR. THIS CAN'T BE WHERE I WAS SUPPOSED TO DIG.
I MUST HAVE MADE A WRONG TURN.
IT'S EXACTLY WHERE WE NEEDED A TUNNEL.
?
COME ON, GUYS.
LAST ONE OUT HAS FLEAS.
I SAID GARFIELD WOULDN'T FORGET US!

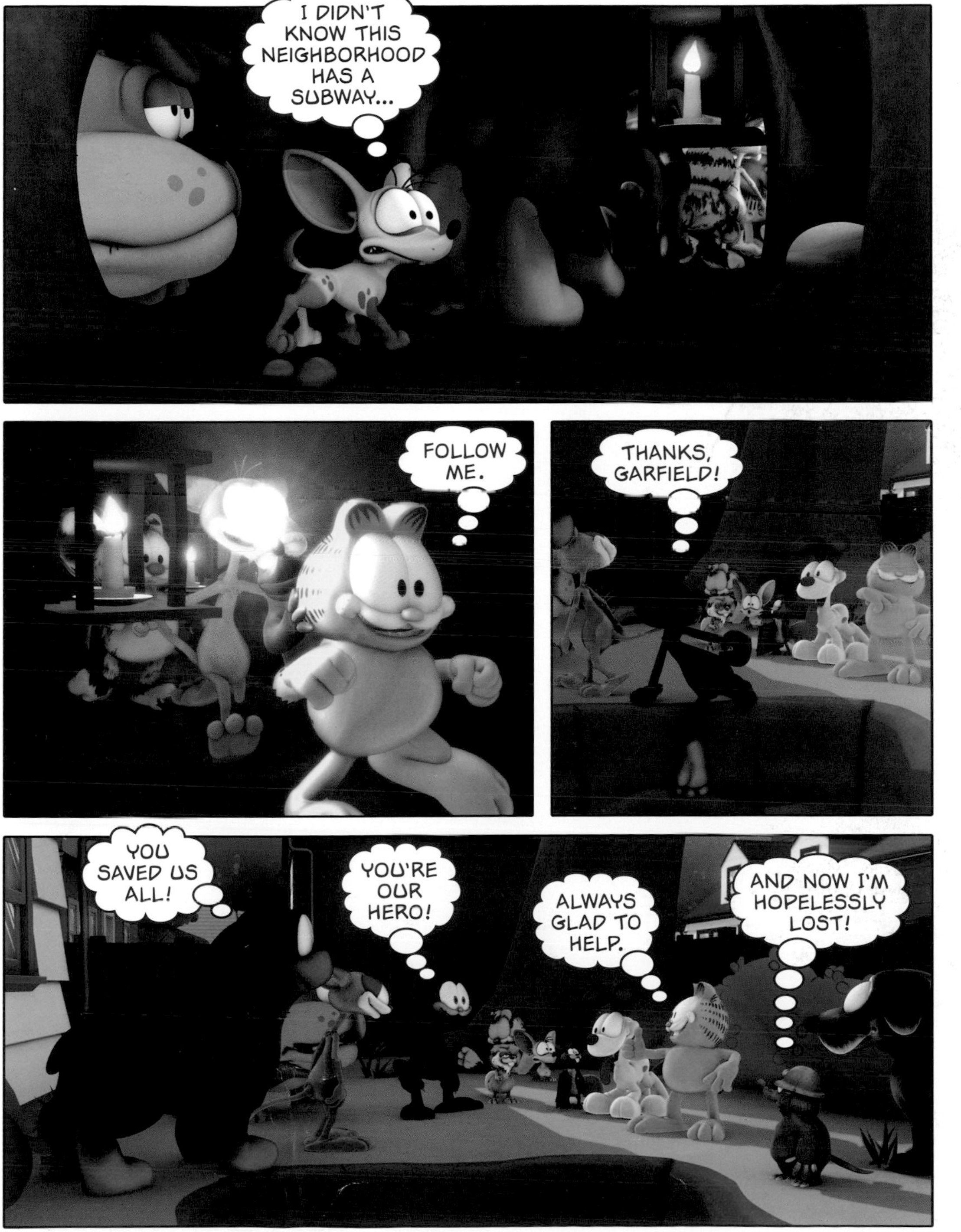
I DIDN'T KNOW THIS NEIGHBORHOOD HAS A SUBWAY...
FOLLOW ME.
THANKS, GARFIELD!
YOU SAVED US ALL!
YOU'RE OUR HERO!
ALWAYS GLAD TO HELP.
AND NOW I'M HOPELESSLY LOST!

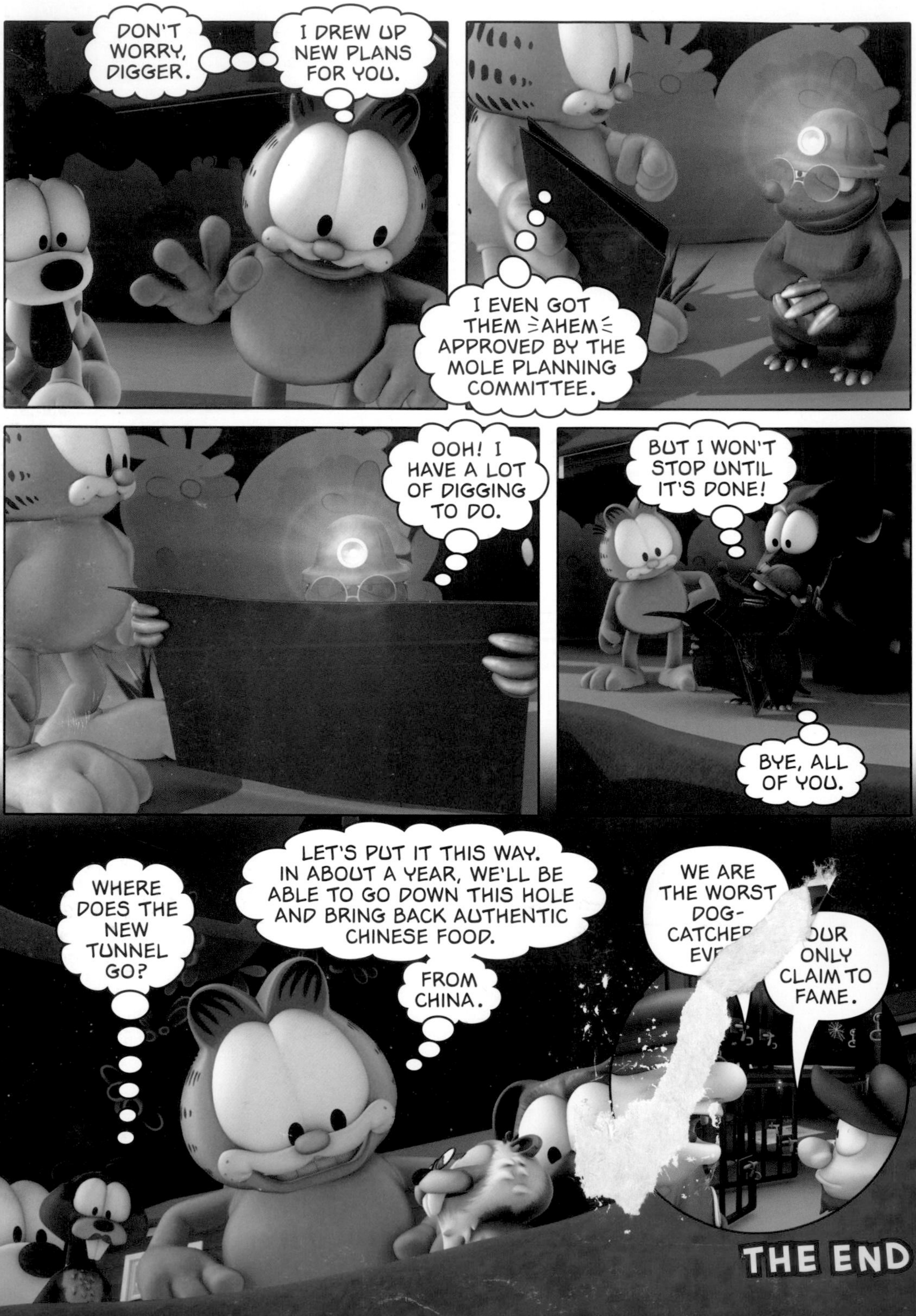

DON'T WORRY, DIGGER.
I DREW UP NEW PLANS FOR YOU.
I EVEN GOT THEM ≥AHEM≤ APPROVED BY THE MOLE PLANNING COMMITTEE.
OOH! I HAVE A LOT OF DIGGING TO DO.
BUT I WON'T STOP UNTIL IT'S DONE!
BYE, ALL OF YOU.
WHERE DOES THE NEW TUNNEL GO?
LET'S PUT IT THIS WAY. IN ABOUT A YEAR, WE'LL BE ABLE TO GO DOWN THIS HOLE AND BRING BACK AUTHENTIC CHINESE FOOD.
FROM CHINA.
WE ARE THE WORST DOG-CATCHE EVE
OUR ONLY CLAIM TO FAME.
THE END